T0208687

THE BOY WHO LOVED SIMONE SIMON

A Collection of Serio-Comic Phantasies

Written & Illustrated by

STEPHEN MOSLEY

authorHOUSE®

AuthorHouse™ UK Ltd.
500 Avebury Boulevard
Central Milton Keynes, MK9 2BE
www.authorhouse.co.uk
Phone: 08001974150

First published by AuthorHouse 03/16/2011

ISBN: 978-1-4567-7636-7

Author Photograph accredited to Dorchester/Ledbetter.

A lifelong lover of movies and monsters, Stephen Mosley played the monster in the movie KENNETH. He's also the crazed Alcoholics Anonymous Leader in ELEVATOR GODS.

Onstage he's portrayed dysfunctional fathers, moonstruck lovers and psychopaths.

He sings with a band called Collinson Twin and lives in a dungeon near Leeds.

For no one

CONTENTS

SPAM FRITTERS

Oh! Spam Fritters, when I eat you with chips,
I love you more than a sadist loves whips.
I queue in the fish shop for what seems an hour,
Just so I can take you home to devour
Your crisp, golden batter and succulent meat,
Washed down with some tea makes my evening complete.
And when the last chunk of pork is gone from my fork,
I open my mouth and get ready to talk,
But as I look around my dark, lonely den,
There's no one to say: "Not Spam Fritters again!"

LOVESICK

Each time I looked at Margaret, a tingling sensation formed in the pit of my stomach. When I stopped looking at her, the feeling remained. Indeed, her very image seemed to be stencilled on my inner-eyelids, as every time I closed my eyes she was there; and every time I opened them, she wasn't.

At night I lay awake, her likeness casting dark shadows across my soul and senses, and my stomach throbbing away. I imagined her arms around me, lulling me into a phantom bliss, so frustrating, so unreal.

Curious things would happen to me in her presence. For instance, I had always thought baked beans to be amongst the filthiest things of this planet, but, to see her eat a plate of the loathsome stuff one morning, I was rather taken by the grace in which they stained her cheek. She was a wonderfully sloppy eater.

During our platonic ventures to greasy spoon cafes on Saturday mornings, I would gaze over her plate of beans and wonder. I felt like crying out there and then: "Oh Margaret, I love you! I love everything about you! I love your small nasty eyes and your shyness and the way you laugh at my sloppy legs!" But I never did. I'd say: "Have you ever licked a battery? Because I have. It can kill you, you know?" Or some other inane uttering, some incapable nothing. And, naturally, she was none the wiser. And I'd walk her to her door and watch her as she disappeared inside, and I'd trudge back alone, through thin sheets of rain, with the hope of 'Next-time' already springing in my heart.

What with the frequency of occurrences such as this, and that relentless tingling in my stomach, I believed this strange new feeling to be love. It turned out to be an ulcer. Or so the doctors told me after I collapsed with giddy weakness one day.

It was all mere conjecture on their part, though, as when they took me to hospital and cut me open, I found I had been right the first time: it was Love. Or so it told me as it crawled out of my belly in the shape of a loathsome goblin.

"Alright, mate," said the goblin. "I am Love."

Oh boy, I thought, *that's all I need.*

It sat at the end of the bed, looking at me, blinking its slimy eyes.

Its figure was hunched; its features all scrunched. Needless to say, I was quite taken aback. The doctors all ran off yelping at the sight of the thing, so, in the absence of surgical presence, I asked the creature if he minded stitching me up again; so embarrassing to be left with a hole in one's stomach. He didn't mind in the slightest and, taking a needle and thread, began to stitch up the gaping fleshy pit from which he had crawled.

As he stitched (not too cleverly I might add) I felt entitled to ask a few questions.

"Sorry, but who did you say you were?"

It smiled at me. Its teeth were like little yellow tombstones. "I am Love," it said.

"Come again?"

"I am Love," it said again.

"Oh, right," I said. "So, what were you doing in my stomach? And how did you get there?"

"I formed in your stomach after you had spent too much time and talk with that girl, Margaret," it said. "My birth was instant."

He was well-spoken, if a little deformed.

"How did you form?" I asked in a tone often found in those who are justifiably curious.

"I don't know, really," it said, whilst biting through an end of thread, "I just did. You know, it's not in my nature to be answerable for my actions."

I looked down at its shoddy stitch-work on my belly and lamented the mess he had made of it. To its defence, I felt sure I spied a glint of apology drowning somewhere in the sallow waters of its eyes.

"Would you rather I had stitched myself back in?" it asked.

"No thank you," I said, without much thought.

As I mentioned, it was a loathsome creature: a real ugly blighter. And I was so shocked by it all that my thoughts began to spill out as spoken words: "If you're Love, which is supposed to be beautiful, why are you so ugly?" It was an insensitive question, I know, but the thing didn't seem too put out.

"Well, what do you expect me to look like? After all, I have been in your stomach all my life. Mind you, I enjoyed being in your stomach. It was very comfortable, reclining in your guts. I used to lie back, reach up and tickle your heart." It made frantic tickling motions with its claws. They were filthy (both the motions and the claws). "It was very nice."

The thing had me confounded. It continued to speak.

"Did you really think I was beautiful?" it asked with inclined head and a flutter of lashes.

I thought for a moment. "Well, no," I said eventually. "I said Love is *supposed* to be beautiful. But it wasn't like that for me. It just meant I slept less, really. And I couldn't eat. And I turned into a total reject every time I was in Margaret's presence. Oh hell. It's no wonder you're such a hideous thing."

"Why thank you," it cooed, genuinely pleased.

"What are you so happy about?" I asked. I was a little mad.

"I'm just happy I was doing my job right."

This blithe gremlin was beginning to annoy me. In fact, it had been irritating me since its moment of birth. "Look here," I said, "how do you expect anything of any substance to occur when you make people act like gibbering idiots?" It was a worthwhile question, one that begged for an answer.

"How the hell should I know?" it said with a shrug of green shoulders. And, with that, the fiendish imp leapt from the bed with an agility that startled me. It ambled off down the corridors. From where I was sitting it seemed to be navigating itself quite well, thus disproving the myth that Love is blind.

"Oi! Come back," I shouted. I don't know why. I didn't want him back.

I was struck with the impression that I had just witnessed behaviour of the rudest extremes. For my part, I felt that during the agonizing time it had occupied my body, I had been a congenial carrier of this character, Love. I had allowed it to fester most affluently, whereas *I* had been reduced to a nervous wreck whilst playing host to this wretched sprite. And now it leaves without so much as a by-your-leave, uncaring that it has most probably scarred me for life with its lame sewing skills. I was most upset.

I lay in my hospital bed, sulking.

Moments later, a shadow fell over me. *Oh not again,* I thought. But it was only Margaret. She'd come to visit me, armed with grapes. I hate grapes.

She placed the offending fruit by my side. "You know I can't stand grapes," I said. I was a little out of sorts after all I'd been through.

"They're seedless," she said, as if that made any difference. I muttered something indecipherable at her. "How are you feeling?" she asked, placing a gentle hand upon my shoulder.

"All right," I grumbled.

She smiled. "I have something to tell you."

She leaned over and I immediately felt repelled and disgusted by the sight of her. I recognised that dewy-eyed look on her face from my mirror. It was revolting.

"I love you," she said to my ear, or rather to me via my ear. I looked down sadly at my scarred, empty belly and then looked to hers, unblemished and snug in her sweater. From behind its purple cotton, within her tummy, I could hear the sounds of hellish laughter, ghoulish and mocking.

"It's all right, love," I said, reaching for the nearest scalpel. "You'll feel better in a minute."

THE BOY WHO LOVED SIMONE SIMON

Flummoxed.

That's what he was. That's what we all are.

It doesn't matter how old you are, or how much experience you have at life, the day will come when, once again, you are flummoxed. First day of school: flummoxed. First day at college: flummoxed. First day on the unemployment line: flummoxed. First day at any new job: flummoxed. Whenever you move house: flummoxed . . .

Any livers of life, whether they like it or not, have to be flummoxed.

Even if you stayed in and hid behind the sofa trying to avoid the flummoxed feeling, it would still hit you. Imagine the first time you had to get out from behind that sofa. I tell you what you'd be: you'd be flummoxed.

And you'd have to eat at some point. After staying indoors for so long and feeding only on things found in the carpet, going out for the first time in ages would soon have you feeling quite (you-know-what).

And even if you decided to starve yourself to death - that would be quite flummoxing; for perhaps the greatest flummox of them all is the day we face our final flummox: death.

You are probably feeling quite flummoxed yourself. I know *I* am. And I'll bet you're all more than flummoxed at the amount of times flummoxed, or some such variation, appears on this page; it's really annoying when a writer keeps repeating a word like this.

I like the word. Perhaps you prefer perplexed, or bemused, but I like flummoxed. But now, in order to save your rage for a worthier cause than myself (as you know, there are many worthy causes for rage out there), I shall try not to say the word again for a while. So now that we are all flummoxed (must try harder) we can relax and know just exactly how flummoxed our hero David was on his first day of the new job.

He had arrived at this job after countless interviews, consisting of much twitching and incoherent mumbling from within an ill-fitting, borrowed suit. Much sweating, much jiggling of legs, much bad technique: that's a job interview for you, especially in David's case. He was at the point where he didn't care anymore. He'd had more job interviews than anyone in the world, and didn't mind in the slightest mumbling at his interrogators that he didn't want the job; he was merely there to satisfy the folks dishing out his jobseeker's allowance. He had no qualms whatsoever in revealing that they were completely wasting their time. Working life was not for him, he surmised. Nor was any kind of life. It all just left him feeling flummoxed.

You see, David didn't really like people that much, or being in their midst, or being in contact with them. People didn't mind David too much, but that's only because they had him in small doses. And that's the way he liked it.

He didn't have a mobile phone like everybody else. He hated the things, and the way that people seemed so dependent on them these days; after all, folk got by all right without them in the 1940's. David would prefer to live like folk did in the 1940's. Anyway, back to his new job.

The interview for this job had been unusual. He had sat facing a gruff man behind a desk. Nothing unusual about that, but the first question to emerge from the interviewer's grizzled mouth was not one of those inane questions like: "Where do you see yourself in five years' time?" – which David believed no one in their right mind should have an answer for: he dreaded to think where he'd be in five years, and always told them so – but the first question to emerge from his future employer's mouth was: "Do you like pies?"

It was a fair question, spoken rather earnestly, if a little unexpected. David nodded in the affirmative, and the man behind the desk rolled a hot pork pie across its surface. David clutched the pie in a confused grasp for the rest of the interview.

It wasn't really an interview as such: the man behind the desk (his future boss) merely rattled on for twenty minutes or so about what they did here (manufacture something or other, David never knew what) and he only asked two questions throughout. You've heard the first one.

"You can eat that pie now, you know," he said, noting the way David just clutched it. David did as he was told, nervously chewing into the gristle. He thought it would be ill-mannered to eat it through the interview, but what did he know? He was just a boy. It was funny how all those manners you tried to show to the world at that age just turned to shit as you grew older and entered 'the real world'. Then the interviewer embarked upon his second and final question.

"Can you swear?"

"Like a trooper," David replied.

"Congratulations, you've got the job."

And with that, they shook hands, smearing each other in pie grease, and the deal was done. After eight or ten months of unemployment, David had a new job.

First day in a new job: *Oh curses, flummoxed again.*

He was led - or rather a nervous stomach on shaking legs was led - to a door.

"This is your office," they said.

It was basically just a room with a photocopier in it. He stood and waited for someone to tell him what to do, he still didn't know. After a while, someone arrived with some documents for him to photocopy. Then, a little later, someone else came in with some more papers for copying.

Oh, I get it, he thought, *I'm the copy boy. Well, that's all right.*

And so it was. Work was sporadic at first, but, over the course of the next few weeks, his duties were extended to filing, ordering stationery and filling the coffee machine. He thought it rather sneaky the way they had piled these chores on him. It wasn't long ago when he used to sit in his office, gaze out the window each day, and think: *Haven't they noticed I don't actually* **do** *anything here?* The trouble was: they had; hence the terrific workload they'd burdened him with. He was even offered a job title – some words with many vaguely impressive syllables that didn't make sense. It should have been 'Dogsbody'. That made sense.

He promised himself he would stay there no longer than three years. Six years down the line, as inexplicable as it was, he was still telling himself that.

It was around his seventh year of working there that he pinned up, against the barren far wall of his office, a picture of his favourite actress, Simone Simon. He thought it would liven the place up a bit, when he wasn't leaping around the office, fencing imaginary opponents with his twelve-inch plastic ruler, and clambering all over the swivel chairs like Errol Flynn may have done, if he'd ever been an office junior. And sure enough, it did.

When he wasn't answering workmates' questions on who she was, he was gazing into her eyes (in between bouts of work, of course). She had eyes that bore deep into his heart, bringing a sweet warm wave of assurance within; eyes that cradled him in the crisp black-and-white world on the other side of the picture, where life was, at least, beautifully lit. She seemed to look down at him and speak in that wonderful French accent: "Don't worry, David. Everything will be all right." And he could believe it from her. She was someone he wouldn't mind co-existing with.

His dream woman used to be Greta Garbo. They were both people who liked to be left alone. He used to imagine himself co-existing with her in a black-and-white dreamworld. "Leave me alone," he would whisper to her at night.

"Leave me alone," she would cry back.

And they'd turn over in their separate beds and roll into an uncomfortable sleep. They would have had lots of fun leaving each other alone.

But then he turned his attentions onto Ms. Simon, and it had been that way ever since. She was in two of his all-time favourite movies: *All That Money Can Buy* and *Cat People*. He'd also enjoyed her in *Curse of the Cat People*. She was beautiful. Strangely, he never felt attracted to any of his fellow earthlings; they all looked the same to him, usually having two eyes, a nose, a mouth, and various other fleshy bits that didn't amount to anything special. But Simone Simon . . . . . maybe it was love. The photocopier had other ideas.

You see, the photocopier was in love with him. This may sound strange, but somewhere within that thing of mechanical parts ran emotions of some sort. David had no cause to doubt. He had noted how the machine would only work for him and no one else. Ever since he began working there, if anyone else tried to copy something, the machine would whirr and buzz and vibrate wildly, whilst tearing and shredding at the papers they wished to copy, mangling them horrifically as they passed through its lovelorn body of cogs and feeders. It was not something that anyone else there ever mentioned. People remained silent on this prickly subject, but David knew they knew. This is why he did all the copying.

The trouble really started when he first put up the photo of Simone Simon. The photocopier then realised it had a rival for David's affections, and began to buzz, whirr, tear, shred and mangle anything that passed through its jealous, electric body. Mulishly, it also began to splatter long dark lines all over anything it did agree to copy.

David took the photo down. The thing worked fine.

Little did it know he had placed the photo of Ms. Simon in a place just outside of its view, but lovingly still in his.

Then, one day, it cut out again. Someone must have tipped it off.

He tried soothing the machine with his fingers, caressing its touch screen display and big green buttons, but nothing worked. It refused to copy, and would only vibrate and sputter toner maniacally, causing anyone near to stand back, shielding themselves with their arms. It would only work when Ms. Simon came down from her wall. It was an experiment David tried several times, and although not a scientific man, he could not ignore the correlation between the photocopier's behaviour when she went up, and when she came down. It was a marked difference in temperament, that was for sure.

David couldn't handle this. He liked having Ms. Simon up on the wall; she made the dull routine of his dreary job all the more bearable. But for her, 'twas a life rich only in paper cuts.

Whenever he looked up and caught her smiling down at him, the world seemed okay. She really did bless the place. But what vexed David further was there really shouldn't have been any cause for the photocopier to be jealous. Simone Simon was, after all, a movie star, as unattainable as you could get for a man of David's lowly talents and grim middle-of-nowhere life. She was also a *dead* movie star. This furthered her un-attainability somewhat. Not that the photocopier took any notice of that. Not that the photocopier took *any* notice of feasible, solid facts.

Although it pained him to admit it, David would never go out with a photocopier. Not just because he was fearful of looking silly: it just wouldn't work. What would they talk about?

And of course, the ugly head of sex was bound to rise at some point, a problem that would have to be confronted. David hated confrontation. Was it even legal for relations to take place between man and copying machine? And if they could reproduce together, what of their offspring? Printed images on sheets of Xerox paper? It was a ghastly thought. David didn't like the idea of being able to crease and tear up his children, throwing them away whenever it pleased him, or whenever they vexed him. He didn't like it mainly because he knew that's what he'd do: whenever they vexed him, whenever it pleased him.

And how jealous would he be when the photocopier was unwell? Big, greasy engineers would have to come round and probe into her innermost parts. How mad would that make him? How sick with jealousy?

He wasn't even sure of the copier's gender. Imagine his horror, as a heterosexual male, on finding his photocopier girlfriend to be really his photocopier boyfriend. It would be bad enough that people would laugh at him for going out with a photocopier, but imagine how hard they would laugh if they found out he was going out with a gay photocopier. Imagine how hard they would laugh.

It went without saying. This was a relationship that could never be, and despite how much the photocopier pouted, it really wasn't that tragic.

One day, he confronted the machine.

He pasted the photo of Simone Simon back in her original place, and watched with exasperated, if not sympathetic fury as the copier whirred and violently sputtered in jealous protest, edging its way towards her with vindictive intent.

"Now look here," screamed David, "I love her! She is the only woman I have ever truly loved, and I am not going to let your sick, jealous posturings ruin our romance – our *uninvolved* romance." He was careful to correct himself.

In reply, the photocopier made stupid noises, as it did whenever anything tried to threaten its relationship with David. He could take no more of this. He felt like a prisoner in his own workplace – even more so than anyone else. He went to see his boss. He was desperate.

On entering his office, the boss looked up from the Western novel he was secretly writing on his computer. It was his dream to revive the Western novel.

"Hi, David; and what can I do for you? Pay rise?"

"No, sir."

"Oh."

"It's about the photocopier."

"Oh!"

"I think it's in love with me."

The boss removed his glasses, and rubbed the nose on which they once sat. He leaned closer. "David, we hoped this wouldn't happen again."

"You mean this happened before?"

"The boy we had before you. He had to quit in the end."

"What happened?"

"The photocopier fell in love with him. It began to make strange noises, refused to copy anything for anyone other than him, that sort of thing."

"That sounds about right."

"I'm afraid there's nothing we can do. It's just one of those things we have to live with."

"But I can't take it anymore. Can't we trade it in for a newer model?"

"A younger girl, eh?"

"What?"

"Sorry. I'm afraid we can't. We still have a year left, at least, on the lease of this thing. As you know, company funds being what they are . . ."

David knew what he was saying and got up to leave, wishing he'd said yes to the question of a pay rise. As he reached the door, his boss called after him. "Oh, David. Just one more thing." He rolled a pork pie across the desk. David watched it with sad eyes as it rolled off the edge and landed with a dull thud against the carpet, scattering a few crumbs as it fell. "Oh well, suit yourself," the boss shrugged, and got back to his Western novel. David left, disgusted.

When he got back to the copy room, he was horrified to find the photo of Ms. Simon trapped in the photocopier's feeder, ready to roll through the workings of its sick, lovelorn body at the touch of a button. "Nooooo!" he shrieked.

A co-worker sat quivering in the corner. "I'm sorry, David," he whimpered: "It made me do it. *It bit me!*"

David understood. He walked slowly and carefully towards the machine with the intention of rescuing Simone from the villain's filthy grip. Suddenly, he saw her beautiful black-and-white face slide through the copier into its filthy inner workings.

"Nooooooooooooooooooo!"

She emerged tattered; long black lines of toner sputtering across her torn and mangled beauty.

David was hysterical. He slammed his fists hard into the copier's vile plastics and yelled and frothed at the mouth. "*You bitch!*" No one did that to Simone Simon. *No one!*

The quivering co-worker was, all of a sudden, embarrassed, and left the office, still quivering, to try and get help. "David's gone mad!" he yelled with concern to all who could hear. At the sound of his frenzied yelping, each co-worker and office dweller looked up from the novels they were all secretly writing on their computers. They left their offices and raced to the copy room.

They arrived, just in time, to see David, in his final flummoxed state, being swallowed by the photocopier. He slid through the machine tie-first and emerged torn, mangled and sputtered with toner on the other side. His red and bloody remains splattered against the ripped mess of the Simone Simon photo.

The co-workers were shocked to say the least, and they all looked on sadly at the torn remainders of these uninvolved lovers. "Ach well," someone sighed, somebody Scottish: "At least he is reunited with his one true love." The others all agreed and went back to their novels. They'd find another copy boy somewhere.

THE FISH

Imagine my surprise on waking this morning to find my arms wrapped round a giant fish. *Funny,* I thought, *that was my girlfriend last night.* But Betty was nowhere to be found.

It's true that, last night, she had complained of itching scales on her back and arms, but I had told her not to worry, whilst feeling quite glad it was not my problem. She had also complained of recurring nightmares involving giant worms escalating in size, and strange women giving birth to malformed prawn-like creatures. But that was no excuse to turn into a fish.

With sad, bulging eyes the fish observed me from either side of its elongated head. Then, parting its rubbery lips, it spoke. "What has happened?" it cried in a wavering voice that very much belonged to Betty.

"Oh my God!" I cried: "It's her. It's my Betty!"

I looked at her for quite some time. I didn't know what to do, what to think. I was certainly having second thoughts about marriage, but what would people think of me? Dumping my girlfriend all because she had transformed into a giant fish. A giant, scaly mass of slobbering fish, which, in protest at what she had now become, slammed its grotesque body against the filth-ridden mattress we had shared for the last six months. It was obscene.

With much hesitation, I scooped her up in my arms. I really didn't like touching her. I raced into the bathroom and turned on the taps (not easy with a fish in your hands). Whilst waiting for the bath to fill, I held her in my arms, doing my best to reassure her. I patted her gills and said: "There, there." Then, when the bath was full, I slung her in. She didn't quite fit. She creased in the middle like a silver banana. Her tail drooped over the other side. Her head propped up the wall, leaving grey wet trails on the tiles. She made horrid gasping noises. Her hideous gills flapped. And I found myself asking for the first time in my life: *What do fishes eat?*

Upon returning from the pet shop with fish food for her, and after fixing myself a sandwich, I found myself thinking: *What should I do now?* All I could do was stare at her, poor girl, and all she could do was look up at me with those fish-eyes so full of fear and misunderstanding: "What has happened? What has happened?" It hurt my mind to hear it.

Suddenly, I had a brainwave. I hit upon the only solution I deemed possible. After a hurried phone call, one news journalist and a photographer trudged doubtfully through the bathroom door. "This used to be my girlfriend!" I exclaimed with curious pride.

They saw not a girlfriend, but an embarrassed giant fish, lolling uncomfortably in filthy bathwater. Both newsmen scratched their heads and cast puzzled looks towards my Betty. I had always been terrified of fish, and more than a little terrified of my girlfriend, I half-joked to the men from the press, who scribbled down my every word disbelievingly.

In fact, they only truly believed me when they actually heard her speak: *"What has happened? What has happened?"* It was then they knew that this wasn't going to be just another giant fish story.

Photographs were taken, and a big story guaranteed with, hopefully, lots of money. I thanked the newsmen for their time, and was just about to get onto the subject of money (and lots of it) when one of them said: "It sure is an unbelievable story."

"It sure is," I agreed.

"And surely the strangest story we have ever heard from a giant talking ape."

As they left, I looked in the mirror and caught the biggest shock I had yet had that day.

THE PHOTOGRAPHERS

"Just a little frost."

Edward Milkley was looking at pictures of graves and feeling envious. He wished his own photographs of cemeteries could be covered with frost, but they weren't. Thus, old George Meat had won again.

He was not a man to be beaten.

The two men met each week to compare photographs. They both shared a liking for the bizarre, malformed and uncanny, and sought these qualities everywhere; from rusted railings, crooked tombstones and gnarled trees, to decrepit buildings and haunted skies – anything within their landscape that suggested it was populated by ghosts. They liked to capture these images on camera, and ran private competitions between themselves to see who could come up with the ghastliest depiction. Meat and Milkley: *Photographers Macabre.*

Meat poured two more brandies from the decanter and sailed smugly across his dimly lit, but spacious chamber. He walked a little more upright than usual, but just a little (his form still took on the shape of scrunched-up paper rescued from the bin). "Just a little frost," he repeated. "It really makes the graveyards look nicer. Of course, I had to get up extra early to achieve the right effect. In fact, I didn't go to bed at all; it was so early, it was still night!"

Edward knew he had been in bed, dreaming of the girl on the 43 bus, whilst Meat had taken these photographs. They were better than his own and he hated himself for it.

The way that ethereal layer of frost dusted the cracked grey stone of the local cemetery almost made one shiver with delight. Edward had shots of the same uneven graves, but these were taken at early dusk, with not a Jack Frost dribble in sight.

He often envied George for his single-minded dedication to their craft. Little did he appreciate that photography was a distraction from the old man's loneliness, from memories of a family he'd long believed dead. George Meat knew a sadness so great that it seemed vital to enforce obscurity about himself.

Of course, at a hundred-and-something years old, George was, to be polite, a little more experienced than young Edward. Indeed, Milkley often wondered how George could ever have reached such a wizened age, especially as he was puffing on what appeared to be his fourteenth cigar that evening (the smoke billowed out of the old man like poisonous gas from an inedible mushroom), and he had never exercised in his life - for fear that his bones might crack.

When the brandies were finished, Meat sent young Milkley away on the same withering lines: "Until next Tuesday, my friend." They were both men who needed privacy; who hid, solitary, behind closed doors. Except on a Tuesday.

With head somewhere between ankles, Milkley made his way down the winding gravel path; away from the large, but empty house occupied by his friend; away from the foul winds that seemed to blow only around that residence. Far beyond lay the town below. The town he thought himself brave to inhabit.

Though the walk was long, and something of a struggle, he made his way back to his dwelling (a one bed-roomed box that balanced on cobbled streets. Sparse puddles of light rippled ineffectively against the gloom). It wasn't so good to be home. The room stank of greying hues. It was, in itself, a scaled down version of his friend's horrible retreat. He didn't sleep easy that night. Through the whirl of thoughts that greeted his head, sleep was naturally uneasy.

He had to take a photograph to better George's. If he could do that, he could do anything. He imagined how great it would be to win: George would value his artistic skill; the world may even love him for it. Better still, the girl on the 43 bus might notice him, and melt at his shy smiles. He knew his sense of the unnatural was just as keen as his sly, scheming pal. So why should it be such a lumbering burden?

All that week he deserted all rest, and walked and walked through the insidious town. He skulked through the cemetery, but found nothing new. He looked all around him with frightened eyes, camera gripped tightly in long, ashen fingers. There was nothing to top George's frost-laden graveyard.

Nothing.

Not even the gloom-sodden clouds that raced through the sky in the guise of shapeless beasts. Not even the grey, human-faced pigeon with shattered beak that stuttered through the earth's bright dirt. No vision could top Meat's.

His best bet looked to be the old willowy tree on the banks of the sludge-like river. Its rough bark was encrusted in the shape of a screaming woman. Its branches brought demons to the senses and mind. Edward reluctantly snapped it, though he knew George would do better. It was as if the old man could *summon* grim things for the camera's pleasure.

Then he heard a splash, and found himself riddled with muck. From the eddying flows of the river's dark meanderings emerged five, six, or seven black shells the size of large dogs.

The huge beetles crept from the water and onto the accompanying dirt track. Their rough legs slopped like distant thunder against the earth beneath. They scurried up into the hills, rumbling manic, an army of depravity.

Edward snapped away hilariously. He lensed the gruesome spectacle in such a way that it filled him with a fantastic loathing. Giddy with revolt, he felt sure he would win the contest this time.

It seemed the world below them quietly shuddered as the beetles passed over it. Then they were gone. In their absence, they left only a petrified silence; and hideous droppings laden with frost that young Milkley also photographed for good measure. He couldn't wait until Tuesday.

Sure enough, it wasn't long until Tuesday crept through time like a broken thief. From the pit of his mansion, George Meat poured another brandy. Smoke guffawed from his eleventh cigar of the evening. He held aloft his startling new photograph in crisp black-and-white. It was so clever the way he had trained the grey, human-faced pigeon with shattered beak to nestle amongst the demon-like branches of the tree in the form of a screaming woman. It was even laden with frost. He liked frost, and could do nothing more than admire the way he'd captured it all against the backdrop of that gloom-sodden sky, where clouds raced by in the guise of formless beasts. He knew he was certain to win again.

He awaited young Milkley's clanging at the door with ever-emerging fever. The clanging came. The fever raged further.

As was Tuesday's ritual, the old man ushered his guest through the elongated door. The two men sat down in Meat's darkest chamber. They appeared less animated than the dust on the walls. By the light of a cold, blowing fire they examined each other's photos.

On viewing Milkley's work, George Meat looked sicker than usual. His countenance revealed shades paler than were ever seen on any spectrum. Milkley had to admit his photos of large beetles were difficult to top.

Then, with much grinding and twisting of withered bone, Meat stood up, revealing his true seven-foot-something length.

He screamed and stormed himself into an electric fury.

The wretched skin, that covered his bones with reluctance, began to fizzle, pop and bubble. It peeled away like rotting paper. Fibrous flesh broke anew through the aged surface. It assumed the shape of boundless clay.

Antennae slithered through his brow, furrowing above eyes of demented sheen. His clothes tore and dribbled away, betraying a body of lumps, stiff and unusual. His figure hunched, hunched - and hunched further to the web-littered stone ground. A crisp black shell rose on his back.

Several spectral, spidery legs tore through his sides and slumped upon the floor, causing small insects to flee in terror.

George Meat had turned into a beetle, just like the ones in Edward's photographs.

Shadows stretched across the saddened building and danced from the speckled walls. The beetle twitched about the room, melding with the dark.

The weight of its throbbing mass was so heavy that it cracked the stone on which it crept. And creep it did; scuttling like a frightened mouse through the elongated door; down the long, winding road that scarred the dark hill.

Halfway down, the raging winds blew the creature onto its back. Its furred crawlers quivered against the light of the phantom moon. With much rubbing of thick legs, it flipped itself over with a shuddering, damp crunch. And then it made its way, roaming towards the town below.

Young Edward Milkley was more than aghast. It wasn't like George to seek out civilisation. He only wished he'd brought his camera.

THE GENIUS

Although not being a genius myself, I did have one living inside my head.

I never saw him. But I could feel him; a smudge of misshapen features rubbing soft against my skin.

And I could definitely hear him. His voice was like an echo of breaking glass, distant and shrill.

I was in my teens when he first piped up. Back then, I considered him to be little more than a figment of my overwrought imagination.

Then, one Bank Holiday Monday in May, he just wouldn't shut up.

I was only twenty-three years old.

He explained that he had taken a liking to my skull, and had decided to attach himself, limpet-like, just living beneath the skin. He told me he was once a great artist and that, with his help, I could become one, too. I told him that was impossible, as I had no artistic ability whatsoever.

"Take some paper and some pens," he said, "and I will show you."

I took some paper, and some pens, and I didn't know what to do with them.

Then, suddenly, I *knew*.

I could feel his presence guiding me as I drew what would become my first masterpiece. It was a girl with a chinless face; a pretty little portrait. Her frog-like eyes would follow me around the room.

"Now you see! You see!" laughed the Genius.

Yes. I saw.

"Now," he said, "I'll teach you to stretch a canvas. And we shall begin!"

I trusted him. Within weeks we had painted about seventy-five original canvases. We painted non-stop throughout that blistering summer. As it was so hot, I often felt like collapsing whilst hard at work, but the Genius guided me on most persistently. I never slept. I rarely ate. The Genius was controlling me, and he was never tired, and rarely hungry.

"Now we must exhibit these works!" he said.

This wasn't such an easy thing to do, but we eventually secured an agent who agreed to bandy the paintings around to important people in the art world. All we had to do was sit and wait. We sat. We waited. It was a tense winter.

By the following spring we had our first exhibition, a small one nonetheless, in a disused office block. Only three people came. Two of them were curious tramps, the other my mother. It wasn't her cup of tea. Even so, I was very proud. The Genius, though, was not.

"We are more talented than this! We deserve more than this!" he exclaimed, slamming his tiny fists against my bones. "We worked hard, did we not? And for what? For *this*? Nooooo! We need bigger! We need better!" This was the first of many tantrums.

"Please," I said, "I'm exhausted. I just need some rest."

"Rest? *Rest*?!" he would bellow. "Who needs rest? Do you see me resting? Nooooo!"

I soon realised the Genius was going to be the death of me.

The Genius had a taste for cheap wine. He made me devour it by the bottle. Day after day I sat in a chair unable to stop the Genius from making me swallow the rotgut concoctions that were his weakness.

"Stop. Please," I pleaded. I couldn't stand the taste of wine, but he forced me to drink. I found myself in a drunken stupor, whilst the Genius continued to have ideas.

"You must paint! You must paint NOW!" he insisted. "You are wasting your life! Time is flowing away! You will be left behind! No one loves you but me! You are not like other people!" His taunts were never-ending.

I continued to paint unsuccessfully. It was a lonely life with just the Genius for company in our squalid little studio. I found it all too easy to slip into an uncomfortable mire of morbidity. I was at my lowest ebb when I met June.

We met, quite accidentally, at one of my little shows. She loved my paintings, which were all portraits of incongruous mavericks like myself. We got talking over some wine and found we had a lot in common. We both liked my paintings, and we both ingested too much wine – we shared lovely, grey-toothed smiles. I grew to like her. The Genius, on the other hand, did not.

For once, I chose to ignore the Genius. I took June out on a number of occasions. Despite the protests of the Genius, I was in love. Soon it came time for me to take her back to my studio - and paint her portrait.

"I won't do it! I won't do it!" The Genius stubbornly refused.

"Please," I murmured. "Please, just this once. For me."

He was adamant. He was not going to paint my lady's portrait. He disliked her, and all women, fiercely.

She stood before me, beautiful, with a bunch of grapes clenched between her teeth, naked save for an old curtain draped over her fully clothed body. She was a work of art in herself. I stood behind the easel, feeling as gullible as I was before I knew of the Genius. There was no way I could replicate her beauty in a painting. Not without his help. And since he was unfairly refusing to assist, I nervously set to work myself. Maybe I didn't need the Genius.

I was wrong. My painting was little more than a stick drawing; a baboon could have done better. June was furious.

"I thought you loved me! How could you paint me this way? Our whole relationship is a sham!" And with that, she thrust the grapes at me and whipped me with the old curtain. She also told me that she had never liked the way I constantly shouted at myself. She found it "disconcerting" – that was the word she used. After snapping the easel over my head, she walked out of my life forever.

I was heartbroken. The Genius was jubilant, and set to work on some new paintings, where he delighted in exploiting my most recent misery.

I was getting fed up with the Genius. Not only did he make me drink excessive amounts of wine, but he also had a liking for chain-smoking cheroots, which made me feel sick. I could feel them rotting my lungs with every reluctant drag.

He also had bad dress sense and made me look like an idiot. He felt most comfortable in paisley pyjamas and sandals, which caused me much embarrassment in the high street.

He also expressed a preference for facial hair; though the weak fluff he made me grow on my chin was laughed at by hairier-faced children. I'd had enough.

"I'm sick of this," I said to the Genius. "Our relationship is all take and no give."

"Oh shut up," he said.

I could take it no more. I set to work on carving him out. I was angry. I had never had any friends, and the Genius prevented me from making any. It was time he came out.

Taking a scalpel, I shoved the blade behind my ear, jabbing it hard against the bone. Instead of the expected screams of death, I heard only derisive laughter from the Genius. On peeling back my flesh, I found only a lumpy, misshapen skull.

"Oh my God," I chattered through my bones: *"Who have I been talking to all these years?"*

With that, I promptly threw myself out of the window.

The local newspaper noted my mysterious death and reported:

SKULL-FACED MAN THROWS HIMSELF OUT OF WINDOW

Hardly an epitaph one accords to a genius.

P.S. If I were really such a genius, you'd have thought I would have found a way out of this box by now.

BEING A SMALL WORLD

Being a dwarf and a writer had never failed to amuse Martin. At times he extracted a slick merriment from the image of his dreary life. Though, most times, he did not.

He sat, day in, day out, in his lonely room, slamming out his soul onto paper by means of a battered typewriter.

The typewriter was centrally placed on the threadbare carpet, its base wedged in piles of fluff and dust. The fluff quivered with every word he banged out.

The curtains were always drawn, lending the room a dark, musty atmosphere, sufficient to conjure those feelings-cum-words. There was no furniture; Martin cared little for material possessions. This was the life of a writer, he assumed. He liked it this way.

Upon finishing a day's writing he would curl up beneath a blanket (actually an old, filthy curtain) and rest his head on the hard floor, beside the overflowing ashtray. He had only taken up smoking when he was finally able to eke out a living from writing full-time. He had seen pictures of Hemingway; cigarette gripped between squat fingers, or dangling from stern mouth, and he liked the romantic image of 'the writer' – smouldering cig butt flailing in his mouth as he furiously typed away. Cigarettes made him sick.

The smell of stale smoke drifted up his stinging nostrils as he tried to rest. Three or four hours later he would fall asleep. Three or four hours later he would wake up. Then he would start writing again; kneeling hunched before the typewriter like a holy man at an altar. The oscillations, caused by the words he typed, resounded and vibrated through the floorboards, and shocked his knees with constant jolts.

Ideas were everywhere; they would attack his brain even in sleep. He always had something on his mind; something he needed to get off his chest.

He had long ago taken to believing the self-told lie that he didn't mind living alone and in solitude; free from the exhaustion of sympathetic glances; severed from the icy tingle of curious glares. He was only a few feet and several inches shorter than everyone else, for Christ's sake! So what? What joy was there in looking at him the way people did? He had never understood.

Once he had had a 'proper job': in an office. It had taken some years and countless rebuffs to secure that job. Who'd have thought that a few feet and several inches could make such a difference to a man's chances of employment? But in this day and age, in these sick times, from the length of a woman's skirt, to the height from which a man's hair stood on his scalp – a few inches made all the difference.

Martin had been lucky to secure that job, and they never let him forget it. Didn't they realise how hard it was for a dwarf to acquire a decent suit? He remembered those days with disdain. He had had a lower desk than everyone else, and his swivel chair was elevated to its highest possible position. He sat there typing all day, imputing data into a computer, craning his neck up at the screen until his eyes went fuzzy and his mind went blank. Those were the days when he had *worked* for a living.

During that mundane time, he had become a cult figure to the witless art students who attended the college over the road. They would show their reverence by gawping in at him through the office window whilst on their fag breaks. He could feel their eyes, young and invasive, blind to their hurt, burning into his every pore and fibre. Outwardly he perspired, whilst pretending to ignore them and get on with his work. Inwardly, he crumbled.

A few feet shorter, that's all, he'd think. *And several inches* – his insecurity was quick to point out. This is what his thoughts were endlessly crying, but he never let it show. And thus, he turned to writing.

To put it simply, if not crudely, one ordinary day he felt bad and let it all out. He wrote it all down. He had shaped and sculpted his indifference into a story. Writing elevated him.

It wasn't a comfortable living that writing carved for him, but it was a strangely contented one. He had saved a fair amount of money from the office job and now earned enough money to pay the rent on his dirty flat, which stood on a street that was maze-like in its similarity to all the other streets that made up the suburban city outskirts. He rarely ate, he often forgot. He was much too busy writing; lost in his self-constructed world of taller people. He preferred it to the world of taller people that existed outside. When he did eat, it was often the greasy, undercooked battered chicken from the nearby takeaway, the bones of which littered his floor.

Anyone who cared to look beyond Martin's stature would see, etched on his face, the look of a man who had taken some rejection. They would see in his eyes a deep and soft longing, flickering jelly-like across the orbs. But no, they didn't need to look deep in his eyes. They had only to see his height.

There goes a man who must handle rejection well, they must have thought as he passed: *What with him being smaller than the rest. And he must handle it so well, what with the way he's just bounced right back and continued to walk the streets, as if he doesn't care that he is a few feet and several inches smaller than everyone else.*

He knew what they thought. These were the kind of people who found no compunction in squashing bugs, just because they were smaller than them and couldn't speak. What if Martin couldn't speak? He was smaller than them. Would he be worthy of a good crushing? The thought horrified him.

He turned to writing as a way of alleviating the routine burden of the job and people in general. He had never been life's biggest fan.

His vast experience of rejection stood him in good stead. He was too used to it by now. It fit his soul snug and easy, like an old shoe.

That's why he wasn't too distraught when his first stories were rejected. They were much too esoteric. Who cared about the loneliness of dwarves? It was all he expected, really; but he kept submitting with steely determination. Appearance was not important in this line of work. He was shielded by words, protecting his diminutive stature and fragile soul. He began to write about people other than himself. He wrote of them all that he knew of them. His characters were shallow, vain, obsessed with appearances and hurting each other. They were bland and largely uninteresting. Naturally, the public loved them.

Martin's stories sold like hotcakes, gaining a cult following amongst several enthusiasts. Horror was his genre, tinged with failed romance: gloom-laden and tragic, but always culminating in a happy, if not complacent ending.

Who'd have thought, thought Martin of his work, *that I, a hideous, twisted dwarf am behind all this garbage.* He was neither hideous, nor twisted – the life of a writer had merely got to him. He was, however, in need of a good bath as his fetid odour suggested. And his work *was* garbage.

He had grown a little bitter in his solitude, and found more and more pleasure in killing his characters off. He poured viscous globules of contempt all over himself, what he wrote, and all those who read it.

Editors and publishers were surprisingly slow in getting back to him once a story had been submitted. That waiting time often had Martin kicking his heels and wondering what the hell he should do next. He spent most of this 'waiting time', when not writing, at the run-down cinema across the block. They screened old classics on a Friday and Saturday night. He sat at the back, alone and unnoticed in the dark, as the projector ineptly flickered black-and-white dreamworlds that swallowed him whole.

The people on the screen were the only giants he felt close to. It comforted him to know that Cary Grant would have been a lot smaller in real life than he was on the screen. *But not as small as you!* his insecurity bellowed.

***God**, if only life was like these movies*, he continually enthused. Then he always thought against it: if his life were like the movies, the strains of humorous bassoon music would accompany him every time he waddled down the street. That's what happened when a short guy walked into a movie. He would not be Cary Grant, scooping up the ladies in his arms; he would be the little guy, sadly looking on at the circus.

***Damn**, I hope that editor writes back soon.*

When the letter arrived from the editor accepting his latest effort, Martin could only feel a transitory joy as he always felt somehow superior to the editors of *Tremble Tales* magazine. They always published his work. Although the magazine enjoyed a strong cult following, even the least discerning reader would question the literary merits of the stories that stained its cheap pages.

What the hell, Martin took his paycheque, bought some rotgut whisky, feasted on chicken, and went to the movies. Then it was time to write again. This was the life of a writer and a dwarf. One day, the monotony of that not so idyllic life was shattered. As he always dreamed it would be.

* * * * *

Being dead and a vampire had never failed to amuse Wally. At times he extracted a slick merriment from the image of his dreary life. Though, most times, he did not.

He skulked, night in, night out, ramming yellowed fangs into human flesh by means of a soulless drive. He reserved all emotion for his actions, other than that of wry amusement – and an inescapable thirst for blood.

He sat, by day, in his dirty flat, listening to the incessant hammering noise made by the typewriter, operated by the dwarf who lived upstairs. At least he thought it was a dwarf, unless it was a child with a large, bearded head; something, perhaps, that he had dreamt up or imagined. But that noise was all too real, all too maddening.

Wally lay back in his coffin, centrally placed on the threadbare carpet, and tried to rest. The dwarf was typing. That hammering drove him mad. He'd smash that typewriter around the little shit's head; until it was reduced to a bloody pulp on which he could feed. Or, better still, he would ram the tiny cretin through the machine like paper, and type hard on its screaming face, before thrusting his fangs into the residual mess.

He dreamt it awake. He dreamt it asleep. He dreamt it at all times. The transition between sleep and wakefulness no longer registered. He existed in a somnambulistic state, unaware of anything but the stale thought of death; draped over his brain like a filthy flannel. Yearning for the rusty tang of blood on his lips.

It was a monotonous routine, the hunt. He'd fix on his arbitrary prey, developing a severe monomania for them before the kill. It could be anyone. Someone he'd spotted from his window, a passer-by in the street. Anyone he liked. A faint feeling of power guided his selection.

For nights, sometimes weeks, he would shadow his victim, closely dissecting their every move with the coldest scrutiny, until it was time to strike. He had never had any trouble blending in. He belonged to no certain fashion: medium build, medium height, no discerning features – just a near-invisible block of suffering, with a numb, starched soul.

In life there had been a long list of classmates and co-workers with whom he remained unremembered. He had never been life's biggest fan. Death offered no further challenge. All he had to do was step from the shadows, alone and unnoticed in the dark, claim a life, take their money, and slip back to the shadows. It was easy. He always felt superior to them. They were just stains on the cheapest life. The dwarf was next; he had stained life for too long and now had to be removed.

Wally knelt in the centre of his dark room. There was no furniture, save for the coffin in which he was buried – he had dragged it to the flat on rising from the grave, figuring it was cheaper than buying a new bed. He cared little for material possessions. He barely stole enough money to pay the rent.

Behind blank eyes, his brain slammed out a baleful mantra:

You type away unaware up there. You dwarf. Little do you know, I am going to kill you, and I am just below you. You needn't bother typing anymore. It will mean nothing once you're dead. You are ignorant to me, just like all the others. But I will strike, and your ignorance will remain. I'll leave it intact, as I freeze it with death. Let it cover you in death as it did in life.

His brain was just one of his distinguishing features.

Over the last few weeks he had followed the dwarf everywhere; he never went that far. He pursued him to the nearby takeaway, and watched him slobber on greasy chicken. He felt pangs of disgust and annoyance at the mess and the noises it made when it ate. Back in the flat, he could hear the bones thud against the floor as the dwarf flung them down. The noise startled his mind from its trance-like state: *I'll kill you for that, Dwarf.*

He followed the dwarf to the movies, but paid no attention to the show. He focused instead on that large, bearded head slumped down at the back, lost in another world. He looked at those black-beaded eyes and felt envious of their wonder.

For three weeks he had stalked the dwarf with careful precision and the utmost anonymity. Usually, he didn't take so long to stalk his prey; he was, after all, prolonging the agony of his addiction, but the dwarf interested him. *What the hell was he typing up there anyway?* Wally ignored his curiosity as he did any other feeling that tried rapping on his brain. He didn't want to find out. He just wanted blood.

The noise of the dwarf's typewriter had become louder, and more relentless than the thoughts in his head. This irked Wally. It was time the dwarf was silenced. In an instant, his taut, frayed nerves let out an almighty snap. The time had come. Before he knew it, he was charging up the stairs, eyes glazed with evil intent, teeth jarring and grinding in his hungry mouth.

* * * * *

Knock. Knock. Knock.

Martin stopped typing the instant he heard it. No one ever banged on his door, not even salespeople, zealots, or other nuisances. This wasn't that kind of area.

His eyes lit up, peering towards the door with great caution. His heart froze. His ears became alert. He could hear the heaving rustle of impatient feet behind the door.

Bang. Bang. Bang.

It was louder this time. He crawled into a corner. They'd go away soon.

BANG! BANG! BANG!

"I know you're there. Open up. Open up, Dwarf."

The words were harsh and metallic, slurring from a garbled mouth by means of a twisted brain.

Martin cowered tighter into his corner. It'd just be a drunkard. There were lots about. And when they've finally got bored and gone, he'd think about moving out of this area and living somewhere safer. Just like he'd always planned on doing. He'd do it. *Just as soon as they went away.*

BANG BANG BANG BANG BANG BANG BANG BANG BANG

The knocking was now constant, growing louder each time. Impatient and invasive; an undeniable intrusion.

BANG *rap-rap* **BANG** *rap-rap* **BANG** *knock-knock* **BANG** *rap-rap*

The intruder seemed to enjoy varying the threatening manner of his knock.

"I know you're in there," he repeated louder. *"Open up!"*

Martin closed his eyes and leaned back against the cold wall, furthering the shivers that ran down his spine. They'd go away soon.

BANG-BANG *knock-knock rap-rap* **BANG**

They weren't going to go away.

All of a sudden: silence. Martin's heart took on an additional freeze. His eyes darted open, fixing themselves on the door. He braced himself. His innards tightened in anticipation. *They've gone. They've finally grown tired and gone.* He knew they would. He knew they would. In just a few minutes he'd crawl back to the typewriter and finish that writing. He'd been distracted mid-sentence. He'd get back to the writing. Once he'd got his breath back regular . . . . . *what was that?*

There was a slight *sscchhhh* sound, scraping against the door, not unlike the unearthly hiss of a serpent. The noise coarsened, growing increasingly vociferous, until it was replaced by a sound not unlike scissors crunching into stiff card – a sound that rose in stridence.

Through the wide crack at the bottom of the door Martin could see carved splinters of wood fall to the floor, gathering by the stranger's dirty feet. *My God! He's scratching his way through!*

* * * * *

And why not? He'd had to scratch his way through a coffin lid and six feet of compact earth upon 'rising' again. Now he'd scratch his way through for his supper. He was very hungry. That ought to scare the little feller.

Martin looked out the window. He felt like jumping. It was a long way down. He knew that the shorter you are, the longer you have to fall. He had learnt that, as he had learnt everything, the hard way, of course. He also knew that the framework of his door was rotten and enfeebled. Even the slightest of men could crash their way through with just a minimal amount of effort. He felt like screaming. But screams went largely unnoticed in this estate. He ignored them himself.

Shards of splintered, rotten wood came crashing to the floor with an almighty creak and bang.

There, stood in the doorway, was a character that could have been torn from the fevered pages of one of Martin's own stories: pale flesh, elongated teeth, bloodied talons, all clad in black. It erupted a sizzling, sweltering hiss as it charged forwards; a blaze of starved addiction.

With heart palpitating wildly, Martin looked towards the one mechanism that had always acted as his defence from the world – the typewriter. He was unusually barren of ideas. He could only think of racing forward and smashing the typewriter into his assailant's balls. His limbs were too weak with fear, though, for him to be able to lift the large, heavy writing machine.

Wally's eyes, lost in the haze of their fiery incandescence, were too focused on his next meal. He failed to see the typewriter, whose vexing noise had brought him to this wretched imposition in the first place. His feet struck the cold metal of the machine. He tripped, his legs flailing over his head. He slammed down hard on the threadbare carpet, amidst chicken bones and cigarette cartons. A pile of fluff quivered upwards on his impact. He found himself coughing and spitting the ticklish nuisance from his parched throat.

Martin turned and ran. Ran like hell. In search of that safer neighbourhood.

Once again, the typewriter had saved him.

* * * * *

The dwarf kept to the shadows. His heart was pounding somewhere between his ears, still frozen in a paroxysm of fear and shock. He felt a strange soreness about his neck. He put his hand up to feel. When he brought it down it was covered in blood. *"My God,"* he cried, *"I've been bitten."* He knew what that meant. He'd written about such things.

He noticed a young man looking at him strangely, then felt a change of heart. *By God,* he thought: *if any of these bastards look at me strangely again, I'll . . . . .*

He cackled fiendishly at his newfound power. And disappeared into the night.

* * * * *

The vampire had finished retching out fluff. He couldn't believe he'd let the dwarf get away. No one had ever escaped him.

Martin had got away with just a small scratch to the neck, caused by Wally's fingernails as he toppled over the typewriter. *Damn typewriter.* Wally kicked it and collapsed in a huddle before it. He began to smile. Thwarted by a dwarf. It made him laugh. It seemed funny.

He tore out the piece of paper that was lodged in the machine. He'd always wanted to know what the dwarf was typing. It looked vaguely like horrific fiction. Wally laughed harder. It was terrible.

He took a clean sheet of paper from a nearby stack on the floor, and loaded it into the typewriter. He began to type: *'Being dead and a vampire had never failed to amuse Wally. At times he extracted a slick merriment from the image of his dreary life. Though, most times, he did not. He skulked, night in, night out, ramming yellowed fangs into human flesh by means of a soulless drive . . . . .'*

By God, he thought, lighting a cigarette from a nearby pack. *This is easy.*

THE CHANEYS

Once upon a time, not so long ago, on that most distant of planets called Earth, there lived three young men. Men who sought solace from shadows; they each held an obsession for famed silent screen legend, Lon Chaney Senior: Hollywood's 'Man of a Thousand Faces'

They had just one face each, but chose to decorate it in a manner accustomed to their idol.

There was Fred Chaney, the Phantom, who taped his nose up with gaffer tape, and drew black circles round his eyes, so his face resembled a living skull, just like Chaney Senior's in *The Phantom of the Opera*.

There was Tom Chaney, the Hunchback, who shoved a cushion up his shirt, wore a wig of matted curls, and glued a cracked eggshell over one eye so he resembled the character of Quasimodo, as portrayed by Chaney Senior in *The Hunchback of Notre Dame*.

And then there was Giles Chaney, the Old Lady, who wore a grey wig with a black dress. He pushed round a pram with a midget in, just like Chaney Senior had done in *The Unholy Three*.

And this was your Unholy Three. There used to be an Unholy Fourth, Pat Chaney, who had adorned the black garb and shark-like teeth of the vampire Chaney Senior had played in *London After Midnight* – but he had got lost somewhere.

They met each Saturday in a little city by the name of Leeds – of Yorkshire, England fame – and sat round a table, discussing their dreary lives over sausages and cigarettes at their favourite greasy spoon. Then, when darkness fell, they would embark to their favourite tavern, the Crackhorse.

This is what happened, one God-given Saturday, when darkness fell, in that little city of Leeds.

Slithering through the streets, like thoughts escaped from a madman's brain, the Chaneys arrived at their favourite pub. They sat in their favourite dark corner and generally frightened the bar staff, bringing ale after ale to their wretched lips. There was one bar maid there they frightened more than the rest. Her name was Stephanie. She was the one they were in love with.

Every Saturday the Chaneys made grotesque gestures, pleading their love (of the unrequited kind) to young Stephanie. (They did this all in mime, of course, just as Chaney Senior would have done on celluloid.) Every Saturday Stephanie drew back in terror. She would never love the Chaneys. She had a boyfriend called Darren. He worked in a shoe shop and had a little black moustache. As the Chaneys full well knew, moustachioed folk always got the girls in the end, yet it seemed part of life's tragic irony for them to fall for the girls of such gents.

As they were each in love with the same girl, a sense of rivalry bubbled within the group. There was much silent hissing at each other from across the table. Fred Chaney lit a cigarette with his feet, just like Chaney Senior had done in *The Unknown*. This impressed no one. To make matters worse, the midget in Giles Chaney's pram was growing restless, so Tom Chaney rocked him gently to sleep. (No one knew where Giles had acquired the midget. It was best not to ask questions.) Nevertheless, the problem of their hopeless desires must be addressed.

"We are each in love with the same girl," lamented Fred Chaney correctly. (Being silent movie star impersonators, they forbid themselves speech, so this dialogue was written on the back of beer mats with a shared black biro. It was either Hell or a mixed blessing when Fred forgot to bring his pen out some days.) "As it should be, only one of us can win the maiden's heart." They were very moral people, despite their idiosyncrasies. "Each of us must, in turn, present a case for our heroine's affections. He who brings the widest smile to her angel lips, wins her love for all time. The others must agree to step down." The others nodded in agreement; this sounded just. Stephanie, however, knew nothing of this sly contest. Naturally, she would have been horrified to view herself as some form of prize for the repellent Chaneys.

No sooner had the challenge been set than Giles Chaney was making a beeline towards the bar with his pram. Stephanie cringed as he neared. Giles plonked the midget on the bar and clicked his fingers. The midget began to dance; a weird soft-shoe shuffle, unaccompanied by music (or shoes). Giles smiled appreciatively, rocking his head to the little feller's movements. Stephanie backed away. Perhaps it was assumed she'd find this act 'cute'? She found it bizarre. The midget continued to dance, until one of his nappy-clad legs, slipping in the grime, inadvertently kicked an ashtray into the air. Ash spilled all over Stephanie's bosom. She was furious and yelled at Giles to get the hell away from her. He tucked the midget under one arm and sank back to his table in a slow, sad movement so unlike the proud, determined march he'd displayed before the midget's dance. The others laughed silently at their friend as Stephanie angrily mopped cig butts from her blouse, using the same rag she used to clean glasses. She was always cleaning glasses when the Chaneys were around.

"Nice trie, Giyules. Illl gow nexxt," said Tom Chaney, who employed an original method of spelling.

Tom, the Hunchback, hobbled to the bar, his tongue lolling from rasping lips. When he got there, he found that he didn't really know what to do. His hunch-backed brain went blank. So he just lurched and shuffled on the spot, grotesquely bobbing up and down. This was no good. It only created creases in his tights. Stephanie beat the wretched hunchback about the head with her ash-stained rag, creating several new cracks in his eggshell eye. He limped back from whence he came. Sobbing into his pint, whilst all his friends both laughed, his eggshell seemed to form real tears as it became all unglued and slid down his face.

Then it was the turn of Fred Chaney, the Phantom. He lurched like a fiend, his cape flapping against his behind like a loose mud shield. He seated himself at the pub piano, whose cracked, and mostly missing keys hadn't been caressed in a long time. His claw-like hands formed made-up chords, and he slammed them repeatedly against the dust-laden ivories. Out came the most thunderous noise imaginable, a strangled requiem he'd composed just for her, hoping it would melt her heart. Stephanie dropped the glass she was pretending to clean, fearing the dirge would melt her ears. The glass shattered by the poor girl's feet; the sound of its shatter obscured by the din.

The Phantom continued to play his malformed serenade. The noise was ungodly. Drinkers clasped their drunken heads; dogs barked in nearby Rodley; car alarms sounded outside; young girls stirred uneasily in their sleep; a tramp fell in the street and gazed at the night sky in wonder; a mushroom cloud erupted over the side-streets of Leeds . . .

Suddenly, Fred felt brusque fingers about his bony shoulders. In one burly effort he was hurled from the piano stool, landing in a carpet of ash and spilt beer. He looked up to face his attacker. It was Darren, Stephanie's moustachioed boyfriend who worked at the shoe shop. He didn't look happy. "Leave my girlfriend alone!" he bellowed at all three fiends, his moustache quivering as he did so. The three goblins shambled through the door quicker than you could say "Lon Chaney Junior". Darren charged after them in hot pursuit.

A high-speed, silent movie-style chase took place through the streets of Leeds.

Stephanie viewed the proceedings from an upstairs window of the pub, and sighed for her lover's return. She watched until they disappeared, swallowed up into night's divine blackness.

Hurtling through the Merrion Centre; racing down Briggate; darting past the Queens Hotel; three lumpy shadows desecrated the damp grey landmarks of the city. One upright, moustachioed shadow gave chase. The moon stared down, blank-faced. Stars peeked through velvet skies.

The hero chased the villains all the way to the canal.

When Darren caught up with the cowering Chaneys, his method of revenge was quite simple: he broke their arms with a callow snap, and hurled them into the canal, pram, midget and all. The Chaneys glugged reluctantly in icy depths, shivering all the way.

Darren smirked and fiddled with his moustache.

A shadow trembled on the water.

Long, taloned fingers broke through the surface and pulled their broken bodies from the stream. Emerging, shivering and damp by the canal's edge, they saw that their saviour was none other than Pat Chaney, their long-lost vampire brother. Darren yelped in fright. The prospect of yet another Chaney proved too much. "I'm leaving," he said. "You guys are nuts." Somewhat unhinged, he raced back to the comfort hopefully provided by the soft warm flesh of his lover's arms.

The three broken–armed Chaneys, and their pet midget, were overjoyed at the sight of their long-lost friend. Typically, they illustrated this with a display of over-dramatic silent gestures using eyes, mouths and feet. As they had broken arms and nothing to write upon, the Chaneys disobeyed their vows of silence, just this once, and spoke in their own withered voices. (They figured it was all right, as their hero had made at least one talkie in his career.) "Pat, great to see you," said Tom, "but where have you been all these years?"

The elusive Chaney smiled, revealing a row of blade-like teeth, and his eyes glowed with reverence as he spoke in a somewhat prouder voice than his brothers: "When a man falls in love, he is lost to the world." And then, from the folds of his dark, toe-length cloak, out stepped Stephanie, the bar maid whom they were all in love with, and who, through no fault of her own, was the cause of all this trouble you're reading. "Friends," announced Pat: "Meet the girl of my dreams." Stephanie smiled, and kissed her lover lightly on the cheek, taking one bat-like arm within her own.

The lovers embraced, like at the end of a film, and the remaining Chaneys' hearts fell as broken as their arms. "Oh well," said Fred Chaney (sad, grey and quiet), a cigarette lit between his toes: "That's show business." It was all he could think to say.

The moon stared down, blank-faced. Stars peeked through velvet skies.

In one depressive melt, Saturday night became Sunday morning in that little city of Leeds, on that most distant of planets called Earth.

WE'LL RUN AWAY

Suzie Schticks. There she is again: the girl of my dreams. All dressed in white, flowing as the sea, cavorting in the waves, the purest thing on the beach, the best thing of this world. As pale as the sands, as bright as the stars, aglow as the moon that shines upon her face: her gentle face: smiling shyly, that lop-sided way. She melts my heart and dazzles my eyes and, oh, her eyes: dark and inviting, gazing in mine as if she sought something there; some refuge from this wicked earth, which is why I look in hers as we dance amongst the surf, and the ocean crashes around us like some great symphony, and laps gently like a goodnight kiss as we lie upon the beach, gazing at that moon, those stars, and then at each other; always at each other. And then she takes me in her arms (oh, those arms) and I take her in mine and we kiss. And melt into each other as if we are all there ever is. And that suits me fine.

One day we'll run away. And get married.

And then I wake up. And go to work.

My longing still pounds in my withered heart, my tears kept in place where they ought to be, so no one can see how I see with sad eyes. But it must be written all over my face. But then no one really looks into my face. Not even Suzie Schticks. Not like she does in my dreams.

I work at the record store downtown. I arrive a little late, as usual, but no one seems to notice. I take my place behind the counter and play my favorite records.

The guys I work with are real nice; I hardly ever talk to them. My boss isn't that nice. He talks to me a lot: "Eugene, go get me some coffee; go down to the store and get me a sandwich. Eugene, play another record for God's sake!" Instead of the one I play over and over, the one that reminds me of her. My name is Eugene, by the way.

No one ever comes into the record store much. Suzie Schticks does, though. Thank God. There she is pulling up at the curb outside, all dressed in black. Her lop-sided smile pierces my heart the minute she enters. Her dark eyes dazzle, but never see me. She is with her two friends, Wendy and Barbie. Barbie's just a nickname; I think her real name is Barbara. The three girls are in a band, The Jemima Sluts. I'm not sure why they're called that, but if some other band were called that I don't think I would care much for them at all, but, as Suzie Schticks thought it up, I think it's a beautiful name. Almost as beautiful a name as Suzie Schticks.

We are quite lucky to live in California, I think. I'm quite unlucky to be in love with a girl who doesn't love me, just as any guy or girl in the same position is unlucky. I'm nothing special. And it's a cruel world. And no passion is crueller, no emotion more agonizing than my feelings for that girl. There she is now, her loving fingers flicking through vinyl. How I wish I were plastic.

She flings a pile of records on the counter. They're by bands I've never heard of. Then she flings some cash at me. I'm not sure it's enough, but I don't mind. I'm much too red and buzzing, like some rare electric fish. She has this effect on me.

And then she is gone again.

She never looked at me once, as if I am diseased with invisibility and meaninglessness, like I feel that I am. The space she once filled is empty and ugly without her. The flesh on my meaningless, diseased, invisible body is a dry, barren desert where her arms ought to be.

I find copies of the records she just bought. Then I put them on. I play them all day. They're not really my taste, but I play them all the same. And learn to love them somehow.

Suzie Schticks is an amazing woman. And when that slow, winding clock finally lets me go home, I dream of her all over again, with sad eyes, closed but gazing, beneath dark, spotted lids. Suzie Schticks: the girl on the beach; the girl of my dreams.

* * * * *

The Jemima Sluts are rehearsing in Wendy's garage. That's Wendy blowing gum on the drums, thrashing them floppy like a girl with eight arms. That's Barbie, or Barbara, on the bass. She looks a bit like Peter Lorre, but that's fetching in a girl. And there's my Suzie on vocals and guitar, and they all harmonize, and oh, what a woman. She really growls out these songs that she writes all herself. They're not really to my taste, but I love them all the same; because they pass through her lips like kisses in the breeze.

Some of the songs are painful to listen to; the ones she wrote about *him*. I forgot to tell you that Suzie has a boyfriend, maybe because I try and forget, but she has, and his name is Mike. And he's a jerk. I don't think she really loves him and I know he doesn't love her.

It makes you wonder: what's the point? I think life is precious but they think life is short. Mike loves his car. Suzie loves her guitar. And somehow they think they both love each other. Or so say one or two songs by the Jemima Sluts. They're not slow ballads; they're more 'up-tempo'. The melodies are nice but the lyrics are awful. I try not to listen. I make up my own words.

I'm outside the garage now, by the way, listening in. I sound like a stalker, or a 'crazie', but I'm not. I'm just a guy in love. I should pass by. I have to get back to work. Suzie doesn't work. She can play music all day, or kiss Mike all day if she wanted, but I prefer her to make music, and I like to think she prefers to make music, too.

The neighbors begin hollering at the noise. They don't like Suzie Shticks. No one loves her as much as I. Her car is on the sidewalk. It looks nice, but I don't know much about cars. I don't drive. Then another car pulls up outside, a bit broken down but very clean. It's Mike. With his permanent smile and sandy-blond hair. Not too short and not too tall, he steps inside the place that I long to: Suzie's garage. There is none of the resistance that I imagine would face me if I tried to do any of the things that man does. The music stops and I feel sick. Just the right mood to accompany me to work.

* * * * *

Girls, girls, girls. I see them everywhere, but, to me, they all look the same as men. The only girl for me is Suzie. She's in every breeze and every glittering wave. She's all I've ever loved.

I'm on the beach now. It's Saturday and I'm not working this afternoon, so I can do these kinds of things. I'm sitting on the sand, a fully clothed rag of bones amid the golden blur of sun-bronzed surfers and flippant lovers. I'm watching Mike and Suzie frolic in the sea. They're a bit rougher with each other than she is in my dreams.

Oh, if only one of these girls around me possessed her magic. If only it wasn't just her who felt so special. If only I was like everyone else. But she is the only one. If I wasn't so insane in love I might ask myself why. But I don't. I'm too full of wonder, mesmerized without logic. I'm in love.

No, I'm glad I'm not like them. I haven't been in the ocean but I walk away as if I've just drowned.

* * * * *

As well as music, we love movies. They're our priority on a Saturday night. We go down to the drive-in; that's our favorite past time when we're not dreaming along to records. I like monster movies best. I can relate with monsters, especially as they don't have girlfriends. If Suzie Schticks ever looked at me, I'm sure she would hiss like the Bride of Frankenstein. But Barbara, her bass player, looks like Peter Lorre, and, as far as I know, Suzie hasn't hissed at her once. Only when she's singing – it sounds like she's hissing sometimes.

We're watching a monster movie now, but it's no classic. Something about a brain in a jar. I'm on my bike, of course; I don't drive. Mike drives. He's with Suzie now. They can't think much of the movie either as they're not paying it much attention. They're making out, and it makes me want to bleed all over their popcorn. Wendy, the drummer, is making out with her boyfriend, Al – who just happens to be Mike's best friend. Barbara is alone, like me; she's just watching the movie. She seems the kind who doesn't mind not having a boyfriend. I think she likes girls. I think she loves Suzie. Me and Barbara have a lot in common. She looks like Peter Lorre. But I can't even get near to her.

The movie ends with blood, noise and kisses, and the cars makes their way to their places above the waves where guys and girls go at such times. I cycle home. And when I dream, I like to think it's purer than the sweat and reality of human togetherness.

Oh, Suzie Schticks.

I'm not even sure that's her real name.

DENTIST

The Dentist is a diabolical man. He runs a surgery in a mansion at the top of a hill where great rains fall and ashen clouds stampede in the sky overhead. He is an evil man. Or so I was told.

One stormy day in July, I found out for myself.

The toothache had been troubling me for weeks. I could see that it was caused by a small cavity, somewhere deep in the back of my mouth. Due to my busy modern lifestyle, I was unable to get round to booking an appointment for some time. Then, when I did, I found myself on a waiting list.

"Are you in pain?" the receptionist asked with more glee than care when I made my appointment.

"Now and again," I mumbled politely, my voice muffled by the intense pain ravaging the insides of my mouth.

"Sorry, did you say you were in pain?" She seemed an impatient woman.

"Yes!" I shrieked.

"Good. We have an available appointment in four weeks or so."

"That would be fine," I lied.

Then she gave me the date and time, and I wrote it down.

Four weeks! During that time, the pain increased. It throbbed and pounded up the side of my head. I only have a small head, so the pain is much worse.

And thus, doubled over, four weeks dribbled by.

I waited in the waiting room, legs all a-jiggle. It was full of sniggering kids who ran amok. I'm sure they were laughing at me, but couldn't see why. Did they think my face unusual? Or maybe it was because I was reading a magazine intended for women - they didn't have much else, and I've always been an impulsive reader. Finally, after what seemed hours of waiting, I was led to the Dentist's office by a pretty, hunchbacked blonde.

The Dentist stood waiting for me. I spied, with concern, the size of his drill (it was a good thing I enjoyed having my teeth drilled). He looked like Bela Lugosi as painted by a drunken lunatic with hooks for hands. He wasn't very polite.

"Sit down," he commanded, like a mad scientist barking orders to his pet ape. This I did. I lay back in the very chair I'd seen Boris Karloff strapped to in Frankenstein movies. He asked me if I would like anything to numb the pain. "No," I said, feeling brave.

"Good," he smiled: "We don't have anything."

Then he drilled away.

The roar ripped the silence to shreds.

The drill broke my teeth to tiny gravels that fell to the back of my throat and choked me. My tongue got caught in the drill's manic whirl. I spluttered.

Above the noise of the drill, I could hear the Dentist conversing with his blonde, hunchbacked assistant. (She was beautiful. How could she work for such a monster?) I don't know what they were talking about, but his eyes were all aglow, so I sensed it was pretty rude. I sensed he was pretty rude, anyway – chatting to sexy hunchbacks when he was supposed to be attending to my mouth. It just wasn't on.

The drill bit was now burrowing into my gums, tearing the tender flesh asunder. I began to gargle on the viscous crimson fluids that gushed from the wounds.

The drill went deeper still. I clutched the armrests of the Monster chair until my knuckles looked fit to pop through the skin. To separate mind from body, to elevate myself from the pain, I found myself chanting arcane words over and over in my head, like *Sarah, Michelle* and *Gellar*, and *Linda McCartney.* This was a drilling I found impossible to enjoy.

After about an hour, the drilling stopped. I was ordered to rinse my mouth out from a cup of water that looked like it had once housed cigarette butts. I spat it out with disgust, watching the contents of my once bone-filled mouth slither down the plughole amidst a meandering flow of blood and brown water.

"That will be one hundred pounds and two pennies," the Dentist informed me, wiping gore from his smock.

I was in too much pain to protest. I just wanted to get the hell out of there. I crushed a hundred pounds' worth of crumpled notes into the Dentist's bloodstained hands. I would have to owe him the two pennies.

Then I got the hell out of there.

I staggered through the streets, my hands holding onto the remains of my tattered mouth. I could feel the ghosts of a thousand drills humming hard into my agape, drooling chops.

Upon reaching home, I looked in the mirror. My teeth were reduced to broken juts of bone, sticking up in sporadic twists from swollen, bleeding gums. The pain was intense. Indescribable.

That night I couldn't sleep. The pain spread through all my teeth and gums and trembled in my ears, up the side of my skull, and even stung like unshed tears behind my eyes.

I raided the medicine cabinet, forcing large painkillers down my throat two at a time. I felt like swallowing the lot. Nothing could assuage the pain.

For the first time in my life, I screamed. I couldn't help it, and I didn't care who heard it. I screamed. But it was no release. I slammed my fists into the wall and cried and screamed and cried. I had never known such pain. It was clear this wasn't going to go down within the customary forty-eight hours.

When I could take no more, I delivered a smashing blow to my jaw with a hammer. I wished to separate it from my face. This didn't happen. But I was successful in removing the remainders of my broken teeth.

I howled in agony.

Weak with hurt, I couldn't even grip the hammer, and I fell against the wall in a weary state. Then I think I collapsed. But although my mind was unconscious, I still felt the pain juddering through my head. I awoke moments later into darkness. And the darkness provided an answer.

The bastard would have to pay for this, like I had to pay for it. He had committed daylight robbery armed with a drill. He had slaughtered my face. All I needed was a wee, but expensive filling, but he'd drilled my entire set out. And charged me for it. This was shoddy dentistry, to say the least. And the least was all I could say through the numb set of swollen jaws he had left me with. I set out for revenge. I had just the idea.

Rummaging through an old drawer, I found my Halloween staple: a set of day-glow plastic vampire fangs. I popped them in my mouth in place of my teeth. They chafed somewhat against the lacerated gums. This would scare the bastard, I laughed in my delirium. Then I set off to the Dentist's mansion atop the hill.

I stormed like bad weather through a cold, heavy rain. I wasn't even wearing a jacket, that's how angry I was. My pain had funnelled into a determinate fury. I leered my fangs at drunkards who happened to be prowling the late-night streets. They didn't seem impressed; their fear probably numbed by too much alcohol.

Finally, I reached the Dentist's abode.

I crawled up the hill, clawing through slops of rain-induced mud beneath dying blades of grass. Upon reaching the gothic structure that was the dental practice, I scaled the wall with chilly fingers, until I reached the Dentist's window. The rain hammered down hard and, accompanied by the wind, tried to knock me from my perch. The elements had probably been summoned to try and destroy me by the Dentist himself. But I was too strong for them.

On quivering, thin legs I peered through the dusty pane. The room within seemed rank and deep with the stench of secrets. Swinging shadows blotted my view. Then I saw him.

The bastard.

I had caught him in the happy act of attaching a large drill-bit to his drill.

I scratched my dirty fingers against the window, and hissed and snarled like a demon, baring my fangs to induce his terror. Lightning forked through the ink-black sky, offering perfect illumination to my horror show.

But he seemed too preoccupied to notice me.

Through the glass, I heard his voice, a wintry murmur, repeating *rat-a-tat* rhythms: *"Cavity, cavity; deep black hole. It's always midnight in my soul."*

The Dentist was huddled over in the darkness, sleeves rolled up, fiddling with the drill.

Whirrr.

It tore into motion.

He held out his arms, resting the spinning drill-bit on his pale veins, his welt-stained flesh. He closed his eyes, threw back his head, and smiled.

Cavity, cavity; deep black hole. It's always midnight in my soul.

I banged on the window to get his attention. He turned, his eyes a lustful blaze. His smile held canines more real and impressive than mine. A slew of crimson gore slopped from his mouth as he opened it and roared with laughter at the pale, toothless fool shivering on the window ledge, choking on plastic fangs (I had gulped them in fear). He raised the drill and shuffled towards me.

I fell to the ground, my limbs powerless to shock, and retched for what seemed like hours in the damp grass, trying to retrieve the plastic fangs from my throat. They came up in a pool of blood and slaver. Then I ran home.

Once home, I beat myself about the face and body with the hammer. I wanted to forget, to beat it all out of me. I yearned to live the rest of my life in dreams; to tear down the daylight and make it black again. Little did I know he would be waiting there, in the black, lurking.

Waiting.

For weeks, sleeping or awake, all I heard was the drill.

Cavity, cavity; deep black hole. It's always midnight in my soul.

Then all was quiet for a while, until workmen started drilling up the road outside my house. I haven't stopped screaming since; but I *have* now gone private.

Every cloud needs a silver lining.

THE WORK OF THE VAMPYRES

"It looks like the work of vampires to me," said Toby. The old man looked puzzled. "Damp pies?"

"Vampires," he corrected, wondering how he could have been misconstrued, especially in light of the bloodless corpse that lay by their feet.

"Oh dear, oh dear. I've heard of those."

Toby had heard of them, too. These days they were all he heard of.

The old man's eyes were pale wet blurs. They looked to the girl on the forest floor: quite beautiful, quite dead - but who knew for how long? "My daughter," he said. Toby placed a gentle hand upon the old man's shoulders.

Another shadow joined theirs on the dead brown leaves. It belonged to Toby's companion, the Reverend Karlston. "Shall I nail her down, Master Toby?"

Toby rolled his eyes; the old man whimpered.

The Reverend shrugged; he got all the best jobs. Removing a stake from his 'tool bag', he tore the wood through the dead girl's belly and embedded her to the dirt. Like his master Toby, he was used to such unpleasantness by now.

And then they waited.

Darkness fell about their shoulders. The moon offered its precarious glow. And within that dim light, the corpse began to move.

The girl writhed in the muck, gurgling in frustration. Pinned to the earth, she could not free herself. The Reverend said a prayer; then Toby hammered a second stake, this time through her un-beating heart. A shower of blood spewed from her face and dribbled down her lips, lightly spraying the Reverend's new shirt. He had long ago accepted that, in this line of work, his shirts would never remain as clean as he liked them. He said another prayer. That over, they beheaded her and walked to the nearest tavern.

The old man shook his head. His daughter's dead head rested atop her carcass, clutched in her own lily fingers.

He felt like shouting after them, telling them to clear up their mess, but he'd had enough excitement for one day. He sighed at the ruin of the young girl's body. Looks like he'd have to bury it himself. In the morning.

* * * * *

The Cock & Bull was not the friendliest pub in Europe, but it was the nearest. Toby and the Reverend felt inclined to blot their jangled senses with cheap alcohol. And who could blame them?

They settled in the tavern's darkest corner and brought a much-deserved tankard of ale to their lips. Oh, for a bosom on which to lay the worries of a restless head; but no, the only females they came across lay bloodless and drained, in a state somewhere between living and dead. By contrast, the girls in the taverns were full of life.

Their thoughts of warm bosoms were disturbed by a frantic outpouring of grief from a man who raced towards them through the open door.

"Please, please," he pleaded. "You must help me. I hear you are my only hope. It's my daughter, she's . . ."

"Say no more," said Toby, slamming his cup to the table. He turned to the Reverend, who was hurriedly slurping the last of his ale in weary anticipation. "It looks like our friends have struck again."

"No rest for the wicked, eh?" laughed the Reverend, gathering his 'tool bag'.

Toby expressed that he was not amused, and they left their ale and dreams of bosoms to the rowdy pub that entertained such pleasantries nightly.

* * * * *

Toby didn't like vampires.

He would never forget the day he'd returned home to find a team of them devouring his family. This left him an orphan. He'd held something of a grudge ever since. With the aid of Reverend Karlston (who had lost his beloved wife, Joan, to the creatures and become demented in the process), he had vowed to destroy their plague.

Toby had a moral heart. He believed it was all right to kill people so long as they had big teeth and drank blood and were, perhaps most importantly, dead anyway.

The Reverend, on the other hand, was merely deranged and, these days, fantasized about sticking his axe into anything.

They may have been amateur human beings but they were professional slayers. There would be no more vampire-induced orphans or widowers. Not if they could help it. The girls of the village would be full of spring again. They had only to find the *source* of all this vampirism; and that was the hard part.

* * * * *

The night, once again, summoned their unique talents.

They were deep in the forest. Lost in the dark.

"Master Toby, what was that?" Reverend Karlston heard a rustling.

Toby heard it too.

They crept onto the dusty track slicing through the trees. Their eyes peered and darted. Black meanderings of darkness wound through the twisted thickets. Through it, they spied a figure racing towards them, arms flailing helplessly, feet burning through the dust. It seemed to be running from the very Devil himself. The two men hid behind a tree. There were plenty nearby to hide behind.

The figure grew closer. From behind their trees, they could see that it was a woman, dressed in a shred of a gown. As she ran, a spill of raven hair furled from her head; her face was damp with tears. The Reverend brandished a small axe from his tool bag. He hoped she was a vampire; he was looking forward to chopping her head off.

As she drew near, Toby pounced. The girl collapsed, a weary weight of bones in his arms.

The Reverend leered and raised his eyes. "Is she a vampire?"

"Shush," hushed Toby. "Let me handle this."

He propped the girl against a tree. Her lashes fluttered, her eyes grew wide. Toby cleared his throat. "Excuse me, love," he said: "You aren't a vampire by any chance, are you?"

She screamed, revealing teeth quite normal in length.

And then she collapsed. The men shrugged, and dragged her back to their squalid dwellings.

The dragging of a comatose girl through the door after-hours inspired a look of quiet disgust on the face of their elderly landlady. But she chose to say nothing. She was much too tired and had already suffered too many distractions from the book she was reading. It was a good one, a real rattling yarn, so any complaints would have to wait until morning.

"We'll put her in your bed," said Toby to the Reverend, resting the girl into the lower bunk. "And you can take the floor."

"Yes, Master," replied the obsequious priest, lying back on the hard rotten creaker of a floor. As Toby rolled into the top bunk and wished him a good night, the Reverend closed his eyes and smiled: he'd never liked having the bottom bunk, anyway.

The following morning, the three awoke early, yet the girl remained silent and would not answer any of Toby's questions. She seemed to be in a state of ineffable shock. The landlady, on the other hand, would not shut up. Her wrinkled old voice shattered the girl's more poignant silence. "What do you think you're doing?" cried the old hag from behind the door. "Dragging young ladies through my door at night. What the Devil's going on? And you, Reverend! A holy man?! I want you out of here. Do you hear me? Out! And take your raven-haired beauty with you, whether she's awake yet or not."

The landlady had finished her book, so now had ample time to shout. She had never liked the way the men stayed out all night, or the way that they came back covered in blood. It was definitely suspicious. She wanted them out. The men had to comply. Vampires were one thing, but an angry landlady quite another entirely. The Reverend would have loved to use his new axe on her, but Toby quietly steered him from this disposition, warning how irresponsible it would appear to hack an old woman to bits. The good cleric was forced to agree. He kept the axe in his tool bag, and blamed his sudden madness on an uncomfortable night's sleep.

They gathered their scant possessions (mainly tools to aid vampire extermination), took the somnambulistic girl by the hand, and left their not-so-cosy dwelling.

With the sun as their shelter, they headed for the forest. Settling beneath a withered oak, they tried to make the girl talk. It was no good. The best they could get from her were stifled moans and terrified grunts.

"Shall I just cut off her head?" asked the Reverend.

"No," said Toby. "This girl has obviously been through something terrible, something awful; something, perhaps, involving vampires. The state of shock that now confines her delicate features . . . well, it looks like the work of vampires to me. She'll talk soon, and when she does, she may lead us to the source of her worries, which, hopefully, will also be the source of ours."

"Please, let me put her out of her misery."

Toby was growing impatient with his impatient friend; he was making him look bad in front of the girl. It didn't matter that she was conked out. "Reverend, there are plenty of trees here in which to embed your sharp implements." And there were. The disappointed Reverend could only hobble with his little axe. He whacked it against a tree in frustration. It wasn't as good as the real thing, though.

Time dripped by. They huddled round a campfire in the fallen darkness. The girl was still insensible.

Toby was, again, reprimanding the Reverend for making foul suggestions. He was calling Karlston a toad. In fact, he screamed the word "toad" so loudly that he didn't hear, from behind, the *rustle, rustle* of parting leaves, the soft, dry crackle of snapping twigs, the patter of cloven feet. A multitude of luminous fingers clawed their way through the veiled dark. The Reverend couldn't help but notice this. "Master Toby, look!" he cried.

Toby turned to see the girl lifted through the gloom. He saw six or seven hobbling creatures carry her away. This was certainly the work of vampires.

It was too late for action. The Reverend had wedged all of their stakes and axes into nearby trees. They were having more than a little trouble retrieving them.

"Stupid man," snarled Toby to his rabid companion, whilst trying to heave a stake from a twisted oak.

"Ah," said the priest. "You only call me stupid because you are in love with her."

"How did you know?"

"I know these things."

The Reverend was right. Although the girl had nothing of much illumination to say, Toby had found himself falling wholeheartedly in love with her. Something had gripped at his heart in regards to this woman, something that he couldn't quite put his finger on. Perhaps it was her raven hair?

Whatever it was, Toby *had* to rescue her from the clutches of these foul things; he *had* to rid the world of their demonic dominion. And he would.

All being well.

He was used to events not going entirely to plan.

As there was little to differentiate between the two men's ailments (one mad; the other in love), they embarked upon an unarmed chase of the Undead, stealing after them through night's cruel dark, up through the sinuous windings of woodland's black heart. They were not too hard to follow or trace, as this variety of vampire seemed to glow in the dark, leaving a stench of the newly rotting deceased in their wake. And the girl wouldn't stop screaming.

Through thickets, thorns, dirt and mud, the two men scurried upon the fiends, until they arrived at a castle in ruins.

"Of course," thought Toby. "Where else would vampires hide?"

The two slayers had wandered past this old castle many a time without a thought as to what lurked within its walls. The vampires slipped inside the building's murk, taking the maiden with them.

"I wish I had my axe," the Reverend whined.

"Shut up," said his master.

The dark skies rumbled, growing darker still. Rain descended at a crashing gallop, and slid down the ruined walls. The two men charged inside after the vampires. It was either that or getting wet.

They were met by a staircase: cold, black, and crooked. It ascended to a darkness so soupy that it seemed, in itself, a tangible, breathing thing. They looked into it, and gulped. They knew there was no other way to go than up.

With hearts racing, nerves jangling, and knees wobbling, they raced up the steps, sailing through the darkness like old ladies dancing. On reaching the top, they crawled through an elongated portal - and found themselves in some putrid chamber.

Hiding beneath the plentiful shadows, hope returned to the moonstruck boy: there she was – that haunting girl. She was tied upon an upright X-shaped frame at the far end of the room, surrounded by gibbering vampires. "You know," said Toby to the Reverend in a whisper: "I'm going to marry that girl."

Talk of marriage always made the Reverend whimper. He had lost his own wife, Joan, so horribly. But he also had other good reasons to whimper: the vampires were hideous. Dwarfish beings in makeshift robes of filth-ridden sack, their large, sodden eyes were like those of a fish. The skin that stretched across their small round heads was grey and tight and would best befit a slug. Their wide, down-turned mouths held cavernous rows of skewer-like teeth, glistening and hungry in the dark. From within the baggy folds of their sack-like sleeves, grey fishy talons crept and wandered towards the girl's innocent flesh. There were about seven of them in all. And all were *hideous.*

She recoiled in slumbering shock, her consciousness slipping even more than her nightgown. Toby couldn't stand the thought of those things touching her, especially not before *he* had a chance. He dreaded to think of her joining their legion. He *had* to save her. He realised now that it *was* love, albeit at first sight. "*Stop!*" he yelled with gallantry galore.

The damned things turned and gurgled at him. Their fish-eyes blazed with a crimson sadness. Toby didn't know what to do. Nor did the Reverend.

"Unhand her, you beasts!" Toby was scared, but couldn't help himself.

The creatures advanced, mouths agape and talons clawed, eyes bulging in fury. One of them spoke. "The girl is ours," it hissed, words slithering from its mouth like verbose snakes. "Leave now!"

"Not without the girl," said Toby.

"The girl is ours," it reiterated. "She is our queen." The others gurgled in vile approval.

"What do you mean? Your queen?"

"Her name is Andrea, Queen of the Vampires."

"But she is human."

"Yes. Long ago, our forefathers warned that we would find our queen: a human woman by the name of Andrea. *Only she* would hold the power to rule over all our kind, a ruler much needed in our godless lives. And her hair would be raven, and she would be beautiful; just like this one here." It pointed a talon at the girl, then continued: "Once we found her, we were to initiate her into our world via an ancient sacrificial rite favoured by our forefathers."

Toby was worried. "What is this ancient sacrificial rite you speak of?"

"We bite her on the neck."

"But how can you be sure she is 'the one'? Sure, she is human, raven-haired and a beauty, but what if she is not your queen?"

"She fits all the criteria. And her name is Andrea."

"How do you know?"

"We asked her."

Toby was furious that these things had the gall to learn his beloved's name before he dared ask. It was a nice name, though; he had to admit. *Andrea*. He let it flower around his lovesick brain. But didn't he have more important things to do? Oh yes. He was desperate. "But it still might not be her," he protested.

"We are quite sure it is. And if not, we shall still enjoy drinking her blood and making her one of us." The creatures all laughed at Toby's dismay: a horrid echo rattling from lungs that no longer pumped. The unhallowed sound ricocheted from the dank, broken stone of their surroundings, a screeching torment, assailing the young man's ears.

Realising that Toby was powerless, the vampires turned back to the girl.

The Reverend, meanwhile, was nowhere to be seen. *Typical. He's run off,* thought Toby, *just when I needed him most.* Not that the demented little fool would be much help, anyway - not now that the creatures beheld the young girl's throat and their black lips hovered above it, their razor-blade canines ready to clamp down into that soft, white flesh . . . Then, suddenly, there rang a cry, rising from behind the frame on which the girl was held. Frenzied and bloodcurdling, it could only be the voice of the Reverend. And it was. *"Chew on me!"* the Reverend shrieked, emerging from behind the upright frame. *"Chew on me instead, you sick little devils!"*

The vampires were, not surprisingly, distracted from their 'ancient sacrificial rite'.

The Reverend had his shirtsleeves rolled up and held out his bony white arms for the creatures to feed on. "Chew on me," he repeated. The vampires looked disgusted and backed away, their sad eyes sullied by the frightful terrors of the Reverend's bone-dry arms. This gave Toby the opportunity to slip forward and try and undo the girl from the frame.

He was having trouble; the knots were bound tight. These vampires must once have been Scouts.

The Reverend's pale limbs seemed to be having more effect than a crucifix at holding these creatures at bay. Then Toby saw why: the Reverend had a long line of crucifixes crudely tattooed down the side of each arm.

"Ho, ho," said Toby. "I didn't know you had those. When did you get those done?"

"I was drunk," the Reverend shrugged.

Toby could quite well believe it, but he was still having trouble with the young girl's tethers. She was unconscious again, so couldn't see how hopeless her hero was at undoing knots. *Oh, bother it,* thought Toby, pushing the frame to the ground in frustration, quite forgetting that his beloved was still attached to it.

Once again, serendipity assisted the hapless slayers: the wooden frame collapsed to the ground and landed atop the little vampires. If Andrea really was their queen, then she had only succeeded in crushing the little bastards over which she held rule.

The vampires were reduced to a slimy, filmy dust on impact, motes of which stained the girl's smooth skin and tattered nightgown.

Awaking to find herself strewn with vampire muck, she promptly passed out for the umpteenth time that weekend. They had the knots untied, eventually.

* * * * *

Days passed, and nights in the little village seemed safe once more, save for the odd drunkard on a Saturday night. But they had learned to deal with the drunk and disorderly before, and they would learn to cope again. The curse of the vampires was no more. The work of the vampires had reached its end. And you'd think that no one would be happier than

Toby and Reverend Karlston, but, on the contrary, they were now unemployed, and, hence, unemployable, again.

As for Andrea, when Toby did finally pluck up the temerity to ask her out, some years later, she turned her saviour down. "I could have been a queen if it weren't for you!" was her tart response. She never did forgive him. She was a shallow girl anyway, thought Toby: it wouldn't matter to her if the whole town were gruesomely vampirised, so long as she was a queen. Yet, he still loved her. Hopelessly. He couldn't help it. Love is funny that way.

Nevertheless, the three of them continued to live in squalid dwellings, with Toby and Andrea in separate beds, and Reverend Karlston taking the floor. He is currently working out means to get those tattoos removed. He feels silly about them now. Even though they saved his life. Life is funny that way.

But who knows? There might come a night when beauties no longer sleep sound in their beds, and the Undead return to feast on all living. The work of the vampires may yet be done. Vampires are funny that way.

PYJAMA BOY'S LAST TRANCE

Imperfect dreams from faded, lost pages. September 2004.

I'm looking for a life that isn't mine: a story with a monochrome feel and a leading lady, a story with a happy ending.

Happy endings? The only ending life allows us is death, and that's rarely happy. So, until my happy death, I have to fill my life: fill it with monochrome feels and leading ladies. But I don't know where to start. This is always my problem.

* * * * *

I love my town. I just hate the people. When they're not talking about wrestling, they only seem to repeat the lame catchphrases they heard on last night's TV. Sometimes they boast of occasional 'shags', but they may as well be discoursing, still, on the tedious mirth of wrestling, whilst I can only yearn for a soulful girl with a winning smile who has nothing to do with this town or its people.

I'm sick of them thinking I'm weird, simply because I talk with shreds of zeal about anything other than the aforementioned subjects. They also think I'm strange because I like to go out in my pyjamas; not to further exacerbate the indifference between me and them, but for personal reasons.

The Fox & Dragon houses all the passion of a squashed tomato on a dusty floor. And from this hole, until the day I'm waiting for arrives, I sit and listen to the same old derision form the same old faces, as fresh to them as it is jaded to me, with a beer in one hand and a cigarette in the other, pretending to laugh until it aches my guts, whilst thinking to myself: *I would rather be sat at home on my own in the dark chewing cardboard.* Then I smile when they don't, and they wonder what for, and I never tell them, and they think I'm weird all over again. And then I go to the bar, where someone will say: *"Nice pyjamas."* It's the same every night, and though 'change' is the thing I fear the most, all I wish and live for is anything different.

You'd think that people would have grown used to my peculiar habits, but people never get used to anything around here; that's why they never leave the town. Everyday they seem to wake with amnesia.

I only stay because I've nowhere to go, and even if I did, the seeking of change seems a futile search. The human condition remains the same, no matter how unique the eyes that view it and the lips that express those views. I seem to find more comprehension in the disordered landscapes of my dreams.

I've withdrawn to these vistas more often in recent years. My cold concrete reality seems further to reach, as if it is dissolving. I'm scared that my world of reverie will soon spill from my head, splashing every horizon in its illusory shade until it's all there is, and home will be a place I'm destined not to find, in this realm or the next.

* * * * *

My brother, Peppy, believes he slept with Drew Barrymore on one of our many seaside jaunts when young. She was really Lucy from Brighton, a fact I learned from being a couple of drinks clearer than he, and she looked more like Lionel Barrymore than Drew. But she told him she was the actress, he believed her, and they staggered to a hotel room. The next morning Peppy woke up in an empty bed with a hangover and a false belief. The hangover eventually went the way of his deceitful lover, but the false belief remained. And now he thinks he possesses some strange ownership over a film star's love. Constantly I'll find him at the breakfast table poring over glossy celebrity magazines, the kind that usually have someone I've never heard of gracing the cover, and his shaking head will emit horrified murmurs of disapproval regarding the suitability of Ms. Barrymore's latest beau.

Then he'll cloud over and remember Brighton, and his tea will go cold.

* * * * *

Music, I always thought, was a way of making sense of things, taking, as it does, dictation from the heart.

Sounds float like clouds and soar like winged serpents through the mists of my mind, in the fog-drenched sphere of my personal Dreamland, where elegies waft along haunted roads, and sigh amongst twisting spires.

I bring the music back with me; I can never forget these sounds I collect in dreams; back to this bed-sit I share with my brother, to this dingy cracked plaster and these black-brick walls. And Sir Arthur Conan Doyle, the goldfish I named after my favourite writer, swims in his bowl, with his googly eyes and useless memory. Oblivion with fins - I envy him all but the eyes.

Peppy owns an ancient multi-track recorder that he never uses, but used to use when he was a member of the Drew Barrymore Experience, a New Wave band from some while ago in which he played bass. He came up with the name, but little else: it seems his whole life is governed by that one carnal experience that never actually happened. Happily, the Drew Barrymore Experience is now defunct, and I sit and hum into the machine that used to capture their rotten sound.

The process is always the same. A series of unsought noises escape my gullet and land, disembodied, on separate tracks. When the noises finally stop I mix them all down in mono, never stereo, and play it back. When that celestial dirge bursts forth from the speakers I find myself shivering, wondering where it all came from. And I forget it came from me. I listen to it again and again, and, although it makes me feel sad and strange, I can't help but like this eerie clamour.

* * * * *

My frequently occasional jaunts to Dreamland have become more frequent and more occasional. This is because I finally met a girl there, and the music seems to haunt me less: all the rhythm I need comes from the beat of her saccharine heart; all the melody I crave spills from her mouth in a whisper, and all her form and grace is one big symphony that itches my heart.

Her name is Lenore, and she glows with an emerald taint (her skin is green). So I'm a bit reticent about inviting her to the Fox & Dragon to meet the people I drink with on a regular occasion who aren't really my friends.

We met in a field in my brain when all was sun and dew. No words were spoken, we just came together, and that was all there was to it: my Dreamland ventures have tendencies towards such schmaltz and flippancy.

We lie in graveyards on sunny days, and I recite to her poetry, but her face remains blank. When I mentioned she had a name from Poe, she looked at me as if I were the one whose skin was green (as if I were daft).

Lenore is not the sole inhabitant of my dreams, but the only one with whom I've formed a connection.

It's a place of shadows, this stage that fills my skull, where the jazz-men trumpet requiems to ascend each sleeping mind.

From eye-corners, I glimpse traipsing Shadows of unknown intent.

I will be familiarised with the shadows soon enough. And I'm not looking forward to it.

* * * * *

The pyjamas were a gift from a sorcerer I know. He lives in the flat above. They slid awkwardly through our letterbox one day, not long after Peppy and I first moved into this tenement. Taped to the crumpled garments was a piece of paper with a word scrawled on it. The word was 'Crab'. It looked like it had been written with a crayon strapped to a child's elbow. Below the ominous scrawl was a phone number. I rang it. Why not? A hoarse splutter identified itself as a neighbour, the pyjamas as a gift, and I as welcome to visit his flat upstairs. So I did.

I thought *our* place was a mess. The floor of our neighbour's dwelling was lost beneath swaying, uneven towers of books. Presumably, they wouldn't fit on the crooked rows of shelves that obliterated the walls. The room was full of gruesome artefacts; ancient, bandaged dead things seemed to lurk in every corner. Suspended from the ceiling was a large stuffed alligator whose gaping toothsome mouth, frozen in silent anger, swung mere inches above my head. And within the viscous, choking air, there huddled a hunched figure in a shroud. A furred scribble of arachnid limbs tore from his waxen scalp, and from this creeping tangle, dead eyes glared white. To my surprise, it moved.

He scuttled from behind a mountain of speckled tomes, looking as if he were part of the grime. As he scuttled, his feet made a startled rap against the uncluttered spaces of the dust-strewn floor. I often wondered what it was that scuttled up here and kept me from rest - and now that I was faced with it, I still wondered.

I thanked him for the pyjamas. He replied in quiet riddles I still can't understand. And that was the start of what Oliver Hardy used to call "another nice mess". From this first meeting, I gathered impressions of my strange neighbour that have never truly evolved.

Known only as the Crab, he's a harmless eccentric who enjoys shouting in public libraries. He also has the great gift of appearing to know everything. One thing he knows is that he feels he has nothing in common with the folk who drink at the Fox & Dragon. When I said that 'neither do I, should we perhaps drink together?' – He told me he didn't drink, and got back to some incantation or other which was probably as useless as my life, but filled with a similar hope. I couldn't help but wonder why he had invited me up there in the first place, but as a respectful sort, I left him to it. Stepping over the empty brandy bottles on my way out.

I am thankful for the pyjamas. They prevent me from sleeping naked and I have always been fond of paisley: I find these curled purple shapes somewhat comforting in a world aglow with barbed indifference. However, I've noticed that every time I wear them, my Dreamland becomes more vivid, and just by sitting still, I can be there as much as I am here.

As my sleeping attire is a gift from a sorcerer, I assume, naturally, that there may be magic woven throughout the threads. This is why I now wear them all the time, and this is why I've begun to appear tolerant of the people and their antics at the Fox & Dragon: thanks to these pyjamas, I can escape them at any time, and be with Lenore at my choosing.

"Pyjama Boy's in a trance again." These are often the last words I hear before I melt behind the eyes.

* * * * *

Time scurries errantly through my dreams. Sometimes I feel I've been away for days, but I'll return to find only eight minutes have passed in the Fox & Dragon, and I'm back from Dreamland just in time for last orders. No one seems to notice I've been gone.

One minute I'll be lying beside Lenore, the next I could be rolling through fields, sliding down slopes, or hurtling through dark empty space awash with sudden colour – I can't put it all down to the effect of this mesmerising girl.

* * * * *

The 'effect' has dissolved, like all other feelings that once were precious joys.

Within the jewelled walls of her softly gleaming boudoir, we lie upon her oval bed – she naked, me in my pyjamas – and I admire her all-over beauty and, occasionally, her green, saucer-like breasts, but when I try to embrace her, she pushes me away and barks in a language I can't understand – this is not merely a sexual advancement on my part, I just have a need for affection, dripping from a life totally starved of the stuff.

Sometimes Lenore lets me hold her fingertips lightly as we saunter Dreamland's tide-lapped shores. There was a time when that was enough: I was just glad to be in the presence of someone I felt needed and understood me, although I've never known *why* she needs me, or *how* she understands.

This lack of contact has begun to bother me – I just want to be held by her. I would give up my life, if the last dream of it were to be spent in her arms. In this dislocated sense it has dawned on me that I don't even know her at all; that I don't know anybody, really.

When regulars at the Fox & Dragon noticed my depression, they intuitively sensed a girl was behind it. This impressed me, so I confided everything with that surprising candour misery brings: "*I'm with a girl I can't understand, she never lets me even touch her, and I'm just plain sick of it all.*" I looked up from my clouded sorrow to find a multitude of understanding faces on nodding heads. They all mentioned similar problems with girls of their own. I was going to ask if they also found kingdoms in their heads to explore, but I could see from their faces they don't. Their eyes are too blank.

People are unique yet remain the same. And that's why I desire to leave this town no longer. It all seems rather pointless. Nevertheless, I'll continue to see Lenore, though I feel lonelier with her than I have ever felt.

* * * * *

When Peppy is sleeping it looks like he's dead.

Because sleep is a process very close to death, it seems inevitable to me that the afterlife, if there is such a thing, must be an everlasting dream. My dreams are as real as

87

yesterday's memories, and as unpredictable as life itself, anything I have felt or experienced in them touches me on some level, and I carry those feelings with me forever after. I have seen nothing in these worlds I could have voluntarily thought or imagined. I don't know from where these images could have sprung.

Sometimes I have found visions so disturbing I awake feeling I have glimpsed Hell, and I lie sweating in the dark, yearning for mercy (for all my unknowing sins, whatever they may be); praying for morning and Her slender beams to raze it all away.

If this is an 'afterlife', why should I be offered such glimpses of it in my 'forelife'?

Visions steal inside my head with swooping regularity, like that dire junkyard of clichés that is my TV. Only, I never know what will happen next. Damn this cold body that ought to be wrapped in someone's arms. Portals gape above my head; they'll swallow me again in the mire of night.

* * * * *

Something. Is. Happening. When I return from dreams to the so-called real world. The change is gradual. I have not always been so forthright as to insist on wearing my pyjamas at all times and places. Several days ago, there was a discolouring of the skin around my eyes and nose. It's now spread all over.

I sense what is happening with undeserved logic. It seems to have stained me, tainting my wakeful life with unnerving fusion. I used to be pale. Now I am green. Just like Lenore. The guys at the Fox & Dragon will have something to say about this, I'm sure. So I'll keep it to myself. Staying indoors. Worrying as usual. Under my sheets.

My brother appeared concerned at first. I've convinced him I've had too much to drink. That's all.

It's all I can come up with in this state. But he believes.

He believes Lucy from Brighton. Still loves him. Somewhere.

* * * * *

I ate the goldfish. Yesterday. The golden shreds of Sir Arthur Conan Doyle's remains gurgle through a system I'm not too familiar with. I've told Peppy that the fish has run away.

I feel wrong. All over.

* * * * *

I contacted the Crab through means no more ethereal than a telephone. He told me to calm down and meet him at the local cinema. Before leaving, I perversely crossed a mirror's gaze. I wish I hadn't. All I could recognise were the two sad eyes, peering out from a body that now assumes the substance of olive mud. I turned those eyes away and hid my transmuted form beneath heavy overcoat and hat.

The rain tears down heavy; it's the kind of rain that still thrashes you wet even when you hide under overhanging concrete for shelter; the kind of rain that seeks you, determined to soak your skin and dampen your senses: the kind of rain that is the least of my worries. For once, I am the most gnarled thing in the landscape, a shuffling blur amidst the downpour, aching all over beneath my hard and reptilian new skin.

The film had already started when I got there. The Crab, a movie buff, was sitting near the back, surrounded by some dark, shapeless friends I'd never met. I sat behind them on the last row, anxious to speak but unable to do so: my every muttering from this malformed tongue was met with popcorn-munching shushes.

I slumped back with no option but to watch the film, whatever it was, wondering all the while why my friend had arranged to meet me in the cinema, when I told him we needed to talk.

Concentrating on the screen, the action tended to blur before me. I took little notice of plot, narrative, or character – I have dramas of my own to contend with – but I did notice how the cinema is very much like the lucid states of delusion I inhabit: it opens like a portal in the dark, allowing those without magic pyjamas to indulge in Dreamlands of others' imagining for two hours at a time, leaving their lives behind them as I do. And when it's over, they step back out into the rain.

The Crab turned to me, speaking in a whisper. "You see the actor up there?" He pointed up to a handsome young thing whose roguish face filled the screen. I did see him; I couldn't miss him. "He comes from a town not far from here." The Crab mentioned the town and I was surprised that someone who graced Movie Land could have come from such a rain-swept nearby abyss. "He used to work in the Co-Op there," he continued. He sat back in his seat and observed the actor with a curious pride; he wasn't as bad as most of them these days. "That could be you," the Crab smiled. I have no intentions of becoming an actor, especially now I am deformed, but I saw his point: sometimes people do come out of nowhere and aid others to see their own visions. When the movie was over, we stepped back out into the rain. And that's what it's all about.

We made our way to an all-night burger joint that I'd never been to before. There was a sign in the window that read: "OUR FAVOURITE CUSTOMER? – SIR

MICHAEL CAINE" – which I didn't believe for an instant. It's possible that someone who looked like the actor could have been spotted eating there once: lots of guys in this town look like Michael Caine circa 1965, but all of them would have been hopeless in *Alfie*.

Nevertheless, the notice only served to remind me further of how indelible an impression those in the acting profession make on we who emote away from cameras, whose dreams remain unseen – and how little impression the stars of our own lives seem to make overall. One has only to think of my brother and the Drew Barrymore Experience; the young actor who had so humbled the rarely humbled Crab, and, of course, the patronage of that burger joint by an imaginary Michael Caine.

The burgers they served there resembled lumps of soft, coal-black meat shredded together like spinach. Nevertheless, I ate one heartily, and so did the Crab. Sitting alone in a sweaty booth, he asked me what the problem was. I told him I was green and, by all appearances, no longer human. It had seemed to slip his attention.

He shrugged as if it's no big deal, as if there are starving people out in this world somewhere who would kill for problems like mine, and, as always, he is probably right.

We said no more about it, my mutation that is, but I told him about my adventures in Dreamland and my girlfriend, Lenore, who, I'm beginning to believe, is somehow psychotic. Again he showed no surprise, and after confirming the accursed nature of my pyjamas, began to rattle on about the importance of dreams and dreaming.

He held up a finger and spoke, in hoarse contemplation, words to this effect: "Sleep is a blatant form of meditation. A bridge between worlds. A dress-rehearsal for death. Your thoughts on a hereafter playing out in your head, and your worries of it spilling into the limbo we currently endure, are well-founded. When we dream, we enter lands adorned by certain overlords or gods. They want us to know they exist, so they prove it to us by nightfall, when they allow us entrance to their chaos. For some, though, that isn't proof enough. For some, there is no more to life than waking and sleeping.

"Bad things can happen in these worlds, just as sure as good things. How else would we learn? If everything was pleasant, if everything was nice? What would be the point? And how much beauty has sprung from misery? And how much joy has sprung from that beauty? It's an ongoing cycle."

I considered his words and all I inherit from the netherworlds described; I've always found it difficult not to believe every word the Crab says; he can be very convincing when he wants to be.

He let out a convincing belch. "All the souls in Dreamland are singing just for you," he slurred.

I hadn't noticed that he'd been supping beer and Scotch all evening. He lay drunk and depressed on the floor, twirling his arms in the air as if conducting some ethereal symphony, a grin on his face and a tear in his eye.

I left him to it. None the wiser.

As I walked home through the grey, beastly howl of this unforgiving weather, I asked myself questions.

Is the Crab a shaman, as he claims, or a piss-head, as he appears?

Does he really know what I'm going through?

Are my pyjamas magic or not?

What is happening to me?

Will the Drew Barrymore Experience ever reform?

Will this rain ever stop?

And then I smiled. You have to smile. People are always complaining about the weather and crap bands.

I'm almost looking forward to seeing Lenore again, though I'm not sure why. But then, what choice do I have?

I only know I'm looking for something but have never found it.

FIN